W9-AFV-440

JARS *of* GLASS

Jars of Glass

BRAD BARKLEY
&
HEATHER HEPLER

Dutton Books

DUTTON BOOKS
A member of Penguin Group (USA) Inc.

PUBLISHED BY THE PENGUIN GROUP
Penguin Group (USA) Inc., 375 Hudson Street, New York, New York 10014, U.S.A.
Penguin Group (Canada), 90 Eglinton Avenue East, Suite 700, Toronto, Ontario, Canada M4P 2Y3
(a division of Pearson Penguin Canada Inc.) | Penguin Books Ltd, 80 Strand, London WC2R 0RL,
England | Penguin Ireland, 25 St Stephen's Green, Dublin 2, Ireland (a division of Penguin Books
Ltd) | Penguin Group (Australia), 250 Camberwell Road, Camberwell, Victoria 3124, Australia
(a division of Pearson Australia Group Pty Ltd) | Penguin Books India Pvt Ltd, 11 Community
Centre, Panchsheel Park, New Delhi—110 017, India | Penguin Group (NZ), 67 Apollo Drive,
Rosedale, North Shore 0632, New Zealand (a division of Pearson New Zealand Ltd.) | Penguin
Books (South Africa) (Pty) Ltd, 24 Sturdee Avenue, Rosebank, Johannesburg 2196, South Africa
Penguin Books Ltd, Registered Offices: 80 Strand, London WC2R 0RL, England

Library of Congress Cataloging-in-Publication Data

Barkley, Brad.
Jars of glass : a novel / by Brad Barkley & Heather Hepler.—1st ed.   p. cm.
Summary: Two sisters, aged fourteen and fifteen, offer their views of events that occur during
the year after their mother is diagnosed with schizophrenia and their family, including a
recently adopted Russian orphan, begins to disintegrate.
ISBN 978-0-525-47911-6
[1. Family problems—Fiction. 2. Mental illness—Fiction. 3. Emotional problems—Fiction.
4. Brothers and sisters—Fiction. 5. Adoption—Fiction.] I. Hepler, Heather. II. Title.
PZ7.B250583Jar 2008   [Fic]—dc22   2007052657

Published in the United States by Dutton Books,
a member of Penguin Group (USA) Inc.
345 Hudson Street, New York, New York 10014
www.penguin.com/youngreaders

Designed by Abby Kuperstock
Printed in USA | First Edition
1 3 5 7 9 10 8 6 4 2

Once again for Lucas and Alex,
with much love

—B.B.

For Harrison—the brightest star
in my universe

—H.H.

Thank you to Stephanie Owens Lurie for her knowledge, her kindness, and her inspiration. Thanks to Peter Steinberg for his encouragement and for being so darn smart. Thank you to Dr. Theresa Vail for making sure we got it right. Thank you to Thomas and Alisa Simmons for answering the phone no matter what time of night it is. Our gratitude to everyone at Dutton Children's Books and Penguin Young Readers for their continuing support.

Finally, thank you to our friends and family.

YOU CAN'T CATCH ME
YOU CAN'T CATCH ME
MY FINGERS ARE CROSSED
AND YOU CAN'T TOUCH ME

—Traditional children's rhyme

JARS *of* GLASS

CHAPTER ONE

Chloe

I THINK THERE are these lies that we tell each other. Like when you go to the dentist and he asks if you floss every day and you tell him yes, even though you know it's not true and he knows it's not true. And, somehow it's just understood or even expected because he knows that you know all the reasons why you should floss, and you know he knows all the reasons why you don't. Or like the lie you tell your father when he asks how your day was, and you say fine or nothing when really Branda, the girl who sits in front of you in English, told you that your hands feel like a dead person's because they're so cold all the time. And when she said it everyone laughed, and you had to pretend to laugh, too, because if you didn't, it wouldn't ever stop and suddenly you'd be known as the girl-with-hands-that-feel-like-a-dead-person's, even though you know it can't be true because you've *felt* a dead person's hands, and they didn't feel like that at all.

The bins at the Wild Oats Market are all arranged by category. All the nuts are together, and the dried cherries are between the papaya spears and banana chips. And all the decaf coffees are at the end of the row marked with green signs so no one accidentally gets decaf when they thought they were getting regular. The candies are all along one wall, like some cubist painting made out of gummy worms and candy LEGO blocks and chocolate-covered almonds and sour watermelon balls. I'm trying to decide between the red licorice swirls and the black licorice swirls and watching as a woman beside me keeps dipping scoop after scoop of English toffee pieces into a plastic bag.

"I really don't need this," she says, letting the plastic door close on the top of the bin. The bag is so heavy that it makes her fingers white where she's holding it. She twirls it twice, letting the top close in on itself before fastening it with a green twist-tie. "I just can't help myself." She looks up at me and smiles, and I realize that she's talking to me, which is funny because no one ever talks to me, except to ask me to pass something or find something or do something. I smile with my lips closed. The smile that I've been perfecting, that says *that's amusing* or *that's nice* or *isn't that interesting*. And I think that's it, she is going to turn and weigh her toffee and walk over to her cart and put the bag in next to her taro chips and her bottles of organic lemonade. But she doesn't.

Instead she tilts her head at me and asks, "Aren't you one of Ellie's daughters?" And just like that, the last eleven months of holding my breath don't count for anything.

I nod, and I know what's coming next. The soft look and the cluck of the tongue and the two words that I've come to hate—I'm sorry. But then instead of closing her eyes, as if my pain is too much to bear, she smiles. "I thought I recognized you," she says. "I haven't seen her in class in so long. How is she?" I keep looking at her yellow clogs. I can hear my father's voice a couple of rows over, having both sides of a conversation about cashew butter and almond butter.

"She's fine," I say, because it seems like the thing I'm supposed to say. The expected lie, the nod when my dentist asks if I floss every day. I glance up and smile, then look her right in the eye, because that's what I also know is expected. You have to make them believe it. It's not that hard to lie to her, because I guess it's not really a lie. She *might* be fine. I just don't know. My father's voice gets louder and I can hear the thunk of my sister's boots. Slow and rhythmic, like a heatbeat.

"Well, tell her to come back. We miss her." I nod again and turn back to the candy bins, even though now the thought of eating makes me feel sick. "Yoga just isn't as much fun without her there." I don't look at her as she loads her cart and makes a slow three-point turn to head toward the bakery section and the checkout. I can hear the sound of Micah's boots now, too, the soft squeak of rubber on linoleum as he walks slowly behind my father. I lean forward and grip the plastic tongs with one hand, stretching the coiled cord that keeps them attached to the bin.

"Come on, slowpoke," my father says to me as they make the turn around the loose teas and into the candy aisle. I pinch half a dozen red swirls and drop them into my bag, then let the top of the bin drop closed. But the noise it makes is loud, too loud. I turn, running my fingers along the top of the bag, feeling the rows of plastic, each fitting into another, sealing the bag closed.

Our apartment takes up the whole top floor of our building. My bedroom is at the front, overlooking the street, just past the kitchen on the left. My father says that my room used to be the servant quarters when this building was filled with the families of wealthy businessmen, living off the shipping industry. It's separated from the rest of the bedrooms, which are all along the back of the apartment, overlooking the garden tucked behind our building, hidden from the street. We got to pick our rooms in order of our age, so Shana went first. I thought for sure she'd want my room, with its window seat and sloped ceiling, but she chose the big room in the back corner with the built-in bookcase. I went next. I was going to take the room that Micah has now, but my father thought that maybe Micah would be afraid all by himself on the other side of the apartment. Of course that was before we'd met him.

The move to Portland was my father's idea. We used to live in an old cape on the other side of Brunswick, right near the ocean. In the summer, we would take our old camp blankets and sandwiches wrapped in waxed paper to the beach for dinner. We'd walk the length of it—exactly a mile each way—every night, my mother and father holding hands and Shana and me splashing through the wet sand, filling our pockets with bits of sea glass and empty mussel shells. When it got dark, we'd walk back home, our flip-flops covered in sand and seaweed, our hands full of stones and seagull feathers. Our pockets too full to hold anything more. Now, there are no more walks. We eat at the kitchen counter, in shifts, dipping bowls of soup or chili from the Crock-Pot set on low at the back of the counter. Shana and I keep an eye on Micah, making sure he eats, fixing him sandwiches and milk to go with his dinner.

I remember in the fall, with the leaves turning orange and gold, we used to walk down to the end of the driveway, where we'd catch the school bus to St. Joe's. Shana and I sat together when we were little, pressed close for warmth, in the seat just behind the driver. Once she was in sixth grade and I was in fifth, she stopped sitting with me every day, preferring most days to be with her friends in the back of the bus, where they would make folded paper flowers, capable of predicting your future. These days we just walk the three blocks over to the City School on Exchange Street. We used to take turns walking Micah to day care, making sure he had his mittens and his lunch, holding his hand when we crossed the street. That was back when our apartment was filled with the smell of turpentine and freshly baked brownies. Now only I walk with Micah every day, making my steps small to match his. Even though she never looks back, I always watch Shana as she walks in front of us, her black scarf whipping across her back in the wind. I keep looking forward, holding Micah's mittened hand tightly in mine as my sister disappears around the corner.

"Chloe, can you please come help put the groceries away?" my father calls from the kitchen. The bed creaks as I stand up. It does that only when I stand up, never when I sit down. Exactly the opposite of what you would expect. My father is standing in the middle of the kitchen on a tiny island of tile surrounded by the sea of double-bagged groceries that we carried up the stairs from the car. We usually bag the groceries ourselves. We make two of them heavy, for my father to carry, filled with half gallons of milk and glass jars of salsa and spaghetti sauce and pickled beets. Four bags are lighter—two for Shana and two for me. Lemons and bananas and mango apricot yogurt and whole wheat fig bars. The last two are for Micah. The lightest ones, macaroni and bread and spinach and black bean chips. It's like the Goldilocks method of bagging groceries. We put them away in silence. Most everything is done in silence here. The quiet has become so normal that it sometimes startles me when I hear the honk of a horn from the street below or the call of a raven flying overhead.

From the kitchen, you can see into the living room. For a long time we didn't own a television, but got a small one finally because Micah was used to it, liked watching it. In the *dyet dom*, where they stored all the orphans, they used either television or a shot of aminazine to keep them quiet. I guess Micah was lucky he got the TV.

"Hey, little guy," my father says. He sounds tired. Micah walks into the kitchen, balancing a plate on the top of his glass. He steps over the mound of empty plastic bags and toward the sink. He might have made it if it weren't for the jar of pickles partly hidden under the mound. I put my hands out instinctively as he stumbles. The plate tips at an impossible angle, sliding from its perch before crashing to the floor. At once Micah is on his knees, fumbling with the shards of pottery still spinning away from him on the tile.

"It's okay," I say, putting my hand on Micah's back. He shrinks under it, pulling away from my touch, as if from something unbearably hot. I see the splash of tears on the floor as his hands scramble at the sharp edges of the broken plate.

"Micah," my father says, softly, kneeling beside him on the floor. "It's okay." A slash of red appears on Micah's hand as one of the pieces catches him between his thumb and forefinger. "Micah, please," my father says, folding his large hands around Micah's tiny ones. They stay like that for several moments before I help Micah stand. "Let's get you cleaned up," I say, leading Micah to the sink. He looks up at me, his eyes still wet with tears.

"It's okay," I whisper. And I wish just by saying it, I could make it so.

I always leave my window open a bit while I sleep. The cold air drifts in, smelling of the ocean and smoke. I can hear the crunch of tires as cars pick their way over the icy cobblestones in the street below, and if I listen closely I can make out the clang of the harbor buoy, echoing off the buildings. Right now I hear a rustling past my door. My father is doing his nightly rounds. He checks on me first, then Shana, and last Micah. I wait, listening to the fading whispers from his slippers and creaks of the wood floor. I pull on my robe, my father's old flannel one, which I rescued from the Salvation Army bag. Meant to hang just past the knees, it puddles on the floor around my feet as I walk down the hall. I hear the door to my mother's studio open and close, then another noise. This one so soft that I might not hear it at all if I didn't know to listen.

Shana is by the door, holding her boots in one hand, twisting her dark scarf around her neck with the other. She bends down to pull on her boots, lifting one foot at a time, balancing carefully as she pulls the laces tight.

"Where are you going?" I ask, careful to whisper.

"Out," she says without looking at me. And really, it's

hard for me to look at her when she's all made up like that, her face so white and so black, both. I pull at the collar of my robe, feeling the chill of the apartment settle around me.

"What about Dad?" I ask.

"You know he never knows," she says, finally meeting my gaze, and she's right. Each night, after making sure the doors are locked and we are all tucked in our beds, he goes in there. I've heard him murmuring to himself, his voice softly rumbling as he walks through the room. I've pressed my ear against the door, listening to the clink of wood against glass as he fingers her brushes clustered in empty Mason jars and orphan coffee mugs. I've heard him crying quietly, saying her name over and over into the empty room.

"Take me with you," I say to Shana. *Take me to wherever you go every night. Take me to where there is noise and light and laughter. Take me to where you forget.*

"I can't," she says, so softly that I barely hear more than a breath of words. And again I know she's right. To take me would be to take what she is trying to escape. She fingers her bracelets, all leather and rubber, except one. The one that mirrors mine and seems oddly out of place. She pushes her hair out of her face, tucking it behind her ears. Both of us used to have hair the color of honey, shimmering in the sunlight. Hers is dyed black, stark against her pale skin. Not the soft black of a velvety cat or the endless black of a night sky. Her hair is flat and featureless, so dark that it seems that if you fell into it, you would be lost forever.

Chloe

We both hear a soft whimper in the dark, Micah having another of his dreams. "I'll be back," she says, reaching her hand toward mine. For a moment, as she touches my wrist, I can almost remember how it used to be. How my mother would pull us tight against her at night to tell us another of her stories filled with dragons and magic and wishes come true. How she would kiss the tops of our heads before tucking us into bed. "My little bookends," she would whisper. She was always between us, holding us together. Now, she is always between us, keeping us apart. "Go back to bed," Shana says, twisting the doorknob. "I'll see you in the morning." The air from the hall is cold on my face. She pulls the door behind her shut with a click.

I hear it again. A whimper from down the hall. My father turns over on the couch in the studio. He is listening, too. He'll stay there all night, curled on the dusty sofa. My mother's old barn coat pulled over him for warmth. In the morning, he will greet us at breakfast, his whiskers and hair smelling of turpentine and mold. Smells that will mix with the scent of cinnamon and maple syrup. It is as if we all lead night lives, separate from the people we are in the light.

I listen for another moment, hearing only the creak of the building settling in on itself as it pulls in from the cold. I float between remembering and forgetting. Halfway between my father and Shana. Some days I feel like I am going to drown in my memories, that I am going to be pulled under by my mother's tide, which tugs at all of us. Other nights, like tonight, I worry that I will forget. That slowly my memories will crack and fade, like paintings left out in the sun.

I walk down the hall to the silence of my bedroom and look at the jars of sea glass lined up on my windowsill, slowly winking in the light from the street below. A blue and green and amber mosaic pieced together over the years, one bit at a time. It became a game in my family to see if we could find a piece of red sea glass, so rare as to be almost a legend. My mother swore one of us would find it someday, when we least expected it. I shove my hands into the pockets of my robe, warming them in the depths of the flannel. I feel something in one of them, something flat and hard. Something rubbed smooth by the sand until its rough edges have disappeared. I take off my robe and hang it on the door without taking the bit of glass from my pocket. As I climb into bed and pull my quilt up to my chin, I tell myself it is probably just a normal piece of sea glass. One that I had forgotten was there. Probably just an oval of green or blue. I tell myself that maybe in the morning it will be gone, just a flutter of a dream that I had. What I don't tell myself is what might be true. That the bit of glass in the pocket of my robe might be red. Because in my family things like that aren't allowed to happen. In my family if you believe in wishes or dreams or magic, you might just end up like her.

Chloe

CHAPTER TWO

Shana

THE WHOLE GOTH thing is so easy it's a joke, and you get bonus angst points if your mother is a lunatic. Mine is. As for the look, think last-minute Halloween costume and you're mostly there—white face, kohl eyeliner, heavy mascara, hair dyed with indigo and henna, no blush. Vinyl or leather skirt, heavy Docs, ripped fishnets, all black. Pierce something. Develop an attitude. Hold an unlit clove cigarette and tell everyone you have to quit. *Have* to, not want to. Listen to whatever's playing, and bitch about it. Bitch about Nine Inch Nails and how cool they aren't anymore. Bitch about everything. Be pretentious. Write bad poetry about killing yourself. Frown so you look bored. Tell people you cut yourself. Have an online nick like Tears_of_ Blood.

The first time I heard *Maine* and *Goth* mentioned in the same sentence, I was like, what? Brooding lobstermen? But no, it's a real enough scene in Portland, and it gets me out of the house. *Develop an outside interest*, isn't that what they recommend when your life starts splitting apart? The usual "they," I mean—guidance counselors and social workers and the pediatrician and the parish priest and teachers and parents and all the other sad-eyed authority types who came around dripping sympathy after everything happened. I like an outside that lets you stay inside. Yourself, I mean.

As usual, I'm in my room putting the costume on, and it looks so damn stupid I almost start to laugh. Like the time Chloe and I dressed up for real Halloween as salt and pepper shakers. Even then I was the dark one. Older by a year, darker by ten. If darkness could be measured. I look at myself in the mirror, which is still ringed by photos of me and Chloe with Mom and Dad, squinting in the sun out at Wolf's Neck Park, going down the water flume at Six Flags with our hands in the air, and the one of Chloe and me holding up the sign at the airport when they brought Micah home. That was just a year ago, but it might as well have been ten years.

"You know what you look like?" Chloe says.

"Please tell me." I blot my black lipstick, then turn my head to fit a safety pin in my ear.

"One of the puppet people in *Zombie Planet*. I saw it the other night on cable, at three in the morning." She lies back on my bed and holds something up to her face, squinting at it, then balances it on her nose.

"Wow, thanks," I tell her.

"Not a compliment," she says, barely moving her mouth, still balancing something on her nose. Weirdo kid. I smile at myself in the mirror, then don't. Once the white foundation and kohl liner are covering me up, a smile looks truly freakish, even for me. It looks like a gash cut across my face.

"That was irony," I say. "Noun. An expression marked by a deliberate contrast between apparent and intended meaning. Got it?"

"I'm smarter than you," she says.

I nod at myself in the mirror. "Yeah, you are."

"Take me with you," she says. The same request she has every night. Right now I can feel my heart starting to rev up, because I want to get out of here. Bad. Dad is starting his rounds, walking the halls like he's decided to haunt himself. Appropriate, since we live in the building that on the ground floor houses the Parson Hills Mortuary. I don't know what Parson Hills means, it was called that when Dad bought the business. Anyone who wants to give me Goth props for living here is just boring and stupid. He sells dearly departeds the way other people sell office supplies. He accepts all major credit cards. The first floor, where services are held, looks just like a church. He furnished it from church supply catalogs with shiny wooden pews and plastic ficus trees and a fountain with an angel that gurgles all the time. I make fun of all of it, but really I like the sound of the fountain. It sounds like coins falling in a distant room, or my charm bracelet jingling. Sometimes I go down there and lie in the dark on one of the pews and just listen to it, fall into the sound. It's weird, sometimes it almost sounds like a trickle of voices, about to suggest something, about to laugh at their own joke.

"Shana, you don't have to ignore me," Chloe says. "I'm not invisible." There is a odd tone to her voice, like she just now discovered she's not invisible and is still marveling at the fact.

I hear Dad moving down the hall, talking to himself. "I just don't know," he says.

I turn and look at her. "Chlo, I know you're not. But I can't take you."

She looks off to the side, her eyes softening, and it's all I can do not to go hug her. But in this getup, hugging, like smiling, seems so out of place it's painful.

"Why not?" she says, and looks down at what seems like a large, bright drop of blood in the middle of her palm, until I realize it's a red piece of glass, the same one she was balancing on her nose before.

"Because you're too young," I tell her.

"I'm only eleven months and fourteen days younger than you," she says. "Not exactly a chasm of years, is it?"

I shake my head and laugh. Chloe and her vocabulary. Like she said, smart. Way more than me. She rolls the glass around in her palm, and her charm bracelet makes a noise identical to mine. What I don't say is that I get into the clubs down in Old Port by passing as seventeen, even though I'm only fifteen. Under the white and black makeup, it's hard to tell, I guess. Chloe, on the other hand, sits there in her Disney World T-shirt and pink Chuck Taylors and jeans with the daisy patch on the knee, and to take her along, even to hang around the water . . . well, I might as well take along the My Little Pony I still have stuck in a shoe box in the back of my closet. Besides, I don't want her there. It's not like anybody is shooting heroin or anything . . . everybody thinks Goths are into drugs, but they really aren't, but still . . . I don't want her around all that black, all that cynicism. Fourteen is a little young to be scorning the world, I think.

"I just don't want you there," I finally say.

"You want me here?" I can hear Dad making his rounds a second time, blowing his nose into the red bandanna he keeps in his back pocket. He blows his nose a lot, a combination of allergies and a broken heart. Over-the-counter meds can only do so much. Chloe holds up the piece of glass and looks through it, closing her other eye to do so.

"Careful," I tell her. "I don't want to have to explain to the emergency room doctors how you cut your eyeball with glass. A little embarrassing. For me."

She smirks. "Thanks for the concern, but you'd have to try pretty hard to cut yourself with sea glass. Smooth, remember?"

"Sea glass?"

She holds it up for me to see, and I look closer this time, the glints of bloodred, the milky edges worn smooth. "Where?" I say.

"Right here, can't you see it?"

"No, smart-ass. Where did you find it?" For half a minute, I can hardly breathe. I remember those stories better than any of the others Mom told us, because they were the ones that came true. Whatever else you can say about my mother (there's plenty), she always had a sense of the dramatic. For three months after we first moved to Maine, she told us stories about sea glass. On the nights it was snowing, she would gather me and Chloe to her, deep in the leather couch, a fire in the fireplace, and pull the comforter up around us. She would open up the front window so that the snow would blow in, gathering in tiny drifts on the sill. As candles flickered around us in the cold wind, she'd talk, her voice all honey and whisper, always about sea glass.

When the earth was still young, everyone lived under the sea, in vast kingdoms that stretched for hundreds of thousands of miles, with mountains three times as tall as any on the land, and chasms ten times deeper than the Grand Canyon. The water was clear and clean then, and light made it all the way to the bottom of the sea, making the ocean alive with fish and coral and shells and seaweed that the people could touch and smell, the smell of salt, because back then people could breathe water as easily as they breathed air, before they forgot how. Angels lived in the water and in the sky, and the land then was only a dirty place for criminals, for people who had been exiled and had forgotten the beauty of their home in the sea. There was no knowledge of death in the water, for those who died were swept away by currents to the unknown parts of the ocean. It was thought that a person simply existed and then didn't; that's how God had made it to be. The kings and queens who ruled the sea were as happy as the people who lived there, with no knowledge of death, no reason to be sad, ever. Not ever. And they were kind. But then one day a bad, bad man came back from the land. He told everyone that he owned the land, and they couldn't have any of it. He made someone, just one other person, want a piece of the land. Then another person wanted it, too. And soon there were fights, and everyone started scrambling up out of the water to own the land, fighting and dying to possess it, to possess each other. To possess everything. Finally the seas were empty except for the kings and queens, who presided over their empty kingdoms, ruling nothing. The water began to grow murky and dark with dirt from the land as people began to dig and build in it, and with the blood of those who were killed in wars over the land. As the kings and queens watched the rain of dirt and blood slowly shut out the light, their hearts were broken. They smashed their crowns against the rocks, breaking them into bits, and the jewels of their crowns scattered in the currents. Even today, so many years later, those jewels will wash up on the beach, blue sapphires and green emeralds and white diamonds. And the most rare of all, girls, is the ruby, the red ruby. For the kings *and queens kept most of those, to remind them of how blood had destroyed their land and everything they loved. To remind them, always.*

She told us those stories for months, all through the winter, until we believed in sea jewels the way other kids believe in . . . I don't know . . . pots of gold at the end of rainbows, buried pirate treasure, something. And then finally, in the spring, she took us to a secluded beach at the end of an island, and there it was, scattered in the sand. Sea jewels. I remember how long Chlo and I just stood, staring, at the bright bits of glass and then at each other, just staring, and we barely dared to breathe.

I grab Chloe's wrist and pull it toward me.

"Ow, Shana. That *hurts*, okay?"

"Where did you get that?" I force her fingers open and look at it, the rounded edges of it, the tiny needles of red light spilling across the white of her palm. "Where?"

"I found it last night."

"Liar. Like you went to the beach."

"Not at the beach." She takes a deep breath, her hand shaking under my grip. "I found it in my pocket. Dad's bathrobe, well . . . my bathrobe now, I guess."

"Okay, let me get this straight. You dig a bathrobe out of the garbage three months ago, and last night you just happen to find a red piece of sea glass in the pocket? That's your story?"

She starts to cry then, the tears heavy and thick as mercury moving down her cheeks, dotting her jeans. "I did. It was just *there*."

"Because obviously Dad hunted for sea glass in his robe, and obviously you never put your hand in your pocket before."

"Shana, stop. It's true. I thought about . . . it's just true." She stops crying almost as suddenly as she started. "Don't believe me. I know what's true." She won't look at me, snatches her hand away as it closes around the glass.

"And I know when you're lying," I say. I hear Dad, in the study, Micah whimpering in his sleep. I shake my head. "I gotta get out of here," I say.

The Bat Club is down on Mercer Street, next to a sandwich shop and behind that toy store that sells all the juggling supplies. They don't even card me anymore, and I never drink anything except water, so it probably doesn't matter anyway. Drunk people are stupid. Anyone who doesn't keep control over their mind is stupid, if you ask me. I don't even like coming here, but you have to be somewhere. I want to be nowhere for a while, looking at nothing, but you can't do that. You can be in the darkest room in the house, with all the lights out. No, you can be in one of those sensory deprivation chambers, like in that movie, floating in salt water the same temperature as your body, with no sound or light at all, and you are still left with everything inside your head, all the bright flashes that wash up out of memory, and you have no choice but to look at them, to look *for* them.

This place is the worst, with a curving bar covered in gargoyles, and rubber bats hanging by strings from the ceiling, everything black and draped in black chiffon and bathed in red spotlights. Like it was decorated by a black widow spider. Really, it's more like a middle-school cafeteria, all the romantics on one side, all the industrials on the other (I'm industrial—no ankle-length velvet dresses for me, thank you). Lots of gossip and stupid crap. Music loud and monotonous. Here, a scream is a whisper, and whispers don't exist. Jason is there, leaning against the far wall with his eyes closed, and so are Magenta and Carmen and Sammy. A bunch of white, middle-class kids playing at sadness and romance.

As I walk up, Carmen grabs my wrist, and I remember grabbing Chlo's wrist earlier, how quickly her eyes rimmed full. "The girl of the hour," Carmen says. "Okay, so you, like, live above a mortuary, and you don't tell anyone?"

"What do you live above?" I ask her.

She looks puzzled under her white makeup, her blue eyes colorless under the red lighting. "I don't live above anything. My mom and dad live in a split-level out in Green Valley."

"And you didn't tell anyone?" I say.

"It's cool, though," Sammy says. His Sex Pistols T-shirt,

I realize, is older than he is. "Do you ever, like, go down there at night, just kind of take it in?"

"Down where?"

"The basement. That's where they do the bodies, isn't it?"

I think for a minute. "You know the best part of living there?" I say. "The door down to the 'basement,' as you call it, is in the kitchen, next to the pantry, and it has a sign on it in big letters BIOHAZARD, all written in red. I see that when I'm making french toast every morning. I mean, you think *your* cooking is bad. . . ."

The way they are all staring at me, I don't bother with the rest of the joke. I sigh. We don't joke, I forgot that part. We stand around, wearing our depression like name tags: HI! MY NAME IS TORMENTED! I shake my head.

"Look," I tell them, when the music finally stops. "It's not scary. Lots of stainless sinks and machines and white tile on the walls and banks of fluorescent lights. Like the emergency room. The guys who work down there go to school for five years. It would be scarier living above a Wal-Mart."

They all just stare at me, the way Chlo did earlier, and for some reason I feel my own eyes filling up, warm and wet.

"Look at us," I say, finally. They do, but not in the way I meant. I see them, cutting their eyes at each other. *Don't set her off.* "Rubber spiders and rubber clothes. We're so *dark*."

I draw out the last word, and the tears move down my face. Now they won't even look at me. "You know what's really scary? A tricycle in a driveway. A mailman walking down the sidewalk. A grocery store. An afternoon at the beach. You know why?" I shake my head. "I gotta get out of here," I say, the same thing I said to Chloe not an hour earlier. Jason calls after me, but I leave the club and make my way down the sidewalk in the dark, under the light of the moon and the streetlamps and the bars, the bits of glass sparkling beneath my feet. Not sea glass, not here. Just the ordinary glass of broken bottles and jars. Bright shards, full of all their ordinary danger.

CHAPTER THREE

Chloe

I TELL MYSELF that it doesn't matter what Shana thinks, but I don't believe it. The sea glass is real, and it keeps being real no matter how many times I walk away from it, thinking it might just disappear. I'm sitting at a picnic table, well, *on* the picnic table, while Micah sits on the swings at the other side of the playground. He wants me to push him. Keeps looking at me with his sad eyes and making weak attempts to pump his legs and get himself moving. Moms and nannies and an old man that Dad has told me like seventy-five times to stay away from are the only people nearby. All the other kids are in the playground, all huddled together in the sandbox or on the jungle gym, or trying to spin each other off the merry-go-round. The two women in front of me are complaining about how their husbands are never home, don't know how to empty the dishwasher, and take off on their bikes every Sunday morning for four hours before coming home and collapsing on the couch in front of football or baseball. I want to tell them they're lucky. The kind of problems they have can be fixed by a marriage counselor or paper plates or cutting off the cable. I want to tell them about real problems, the ones that keep you awake at night and make you whimper in your sleep or haunt the halls in the dark hours of morning. Nothing can solve those. Not medication or talk therapy or macramé. Not even love. I want to tell them you need to hold the good things in your hands and look at them and touch them and breathe them in. Sometimes things feel so perfect that you almost can't believe they're real. And suddenly they're not.

I can always hear Micah's voice, even from where I am sitting on the picnic table, surrounded by the buzz of women talking. Maybe it's because he doesn't speak English very well, so the sound is unique. Or maybe it's because he doesn't speak very often, so when he does, I always notice. In Russia, the ones who talked too much, who stood out, got sent to the hospital, the *psikhushka*, for discipline—or as they liked to call it "psychiatric care."

I watch him try to pump, resolving to let him try for a few more minutes before I help him. Then I see the boys approaching him from the rear, and I push myself to standing. I don't know these boys, but I know the type, the way they walk, practicing the swagger of their older brothers or bad guys on television. There are three of them. They always travel in groups of three or more. They ring Micah,

Chloe

actually circling him like a pack of animals. And, like in nature, they have found the weakest member of the herd. Words like *freak* and *weirdo* float toward me. The soft words of elementary school boys that somehow hurt more than fists. *If only* . . . I think, regretting never being where I am needed in time. As I run past the merry-go-round to the swings, children whip past, half laughing half screaming.

"Get out of here," I say to the one nearest me. He sneers, but I guess I am just old enough to get them going. One gives me the finger as he walks away. Nice.

"Chloe." The way Micah says it, it sounds like two words. *Chlo-ee.* Then, "Push . . . please." I walk behind him and grab both chains in my hands. I pull him toward me slightly, feeling his weight against my fingers as I lift him to get him started. Then I let go, letting him fall away from me in an arc, before rising again. I step back and push.

"Pump your legs," I tell him, and he does, but only a little, because he knows I'll keep pushing. I always do.

The packet they sent to my parents said that he could speak some English. They found out different when they first met him, but as my dad said, it's not like a bad steak dinner. You don't send a kid back just because it's not what you expected. I guess what the people at the *dyet dom* meant by "some English" was a handful of words. *Hello. Thank you.* Although inexplicably he could say, *I would like to have some french toast, please.* He'd only been with us a few months before my mother really started to slide and only a few more before she was hospitalized. Barely time to know her before she became the other her. The social worker said that they could find another home for him . . . *considering*. And she said it just like that. As if she couldn't bring herself to say it aloud. *We can take him back*, she said, like he was a sweater or a bracelet. My father said no. Micah's part of our family.

I keep pushing, shifting my weight back and forth to follow the rhythm of the swing. Micah likes to go high, really high. Until the chains go slack on the upswing before gravity takes over, pulling him back, snapping the chains tight again as he falls.

The decision to adopt him was a family one. *We all have to be on board with this one*, my mother said. *He's going to need all of us.* At the time none of us knew how much. We had just moved to Portland, the first step in what I now think of as my father's way of coping with my mother's illness. Like stepping-stones across a fast moving stream, he tried to find dry places for us to land, where we could rest a bit before we were forced to step out again, each time testing our balance. Micah was another stone. Art classes another. I watched him try to string together enough stones to get us to the other side, to try and keep us safe. How could any of us know that there wasn't another side? As least not for my mother.

"We should go," I say to Micah as he swings back toward me. I use my arms to absorb Micah's weight, slowing him down. He stops pumping and drags his sneakers in the

Chloe

wood chips under the swing, sending a fine dust swirling up around his ankles. "Should we go get ice cream?" I ask as he stands up, his legs uncertain after swinging for so long. I start to pantomime a cone, but Micah knows this one. *He'll learn what he needs to,* the social worker told us. *Or what he wants to.*

I hold his hand as we cross the street and start walking toward the water. It's cold in the shade of the buildings, making me shiver. "You sure?" I ask, feeling the cold of his fingers. It's warmer than it has been lately, but it's still fall, late fall, and the wind off the ocean feels icy and damp.

"Yes," he says, squeezing my hand. "Please," he says, looking up at me. We have to cross two more streets before we reach the Ice House. I can see the sun dipping farther as we cross each street, as if it only falls when it is hidden behind the buildings.

"Chocolate?" I ask, hanging my coat over the back of my chair. He nods then does the same and sits across from me. "Be right back." The counter is old and scarred with initials forever linked inside the borders of hearts.

"Hey there, Chloe," the woman behind the counter says. I don't know her name, but she knows mine. Having a family like mine gives you a perverse sort of notoriety. "What'll it be?" She lifts her hand in greeting at Micah, who waves slightly at her before looking back down at his hands.

"Two chocolates," I say. "Sugar cones, please." Outside the garbage truck rumbles to a stop in front of the shop. Out spill two men, one lifting the cans on our side of the street. The other cutting through traffic to the other side.

"Damn it," she says, the scoop suspended in one hand. "They left it again." I look out at the curb, but all I see are three trash cans. Two big green ones with wheels and a small silver metal one. The kind Oscar the Grouch lives in.

"They left what?" I ask, watching as she pushes a scoop on one cone before diving into the bin for another.

"Do you know what the hardest thing to throw away is?" she asks, as if she hadn't heard my question. I shake my head, then dig in my coat pocket for the five my father gave me. "A trash can." I look back to the curb, where the cans sit. "I've been trying to get them to take that one away for weeks," she says. "The bottom's rusted clear through." She hands me the cones and takes my money, turning toward the cash register. I walk over and give Micah his cone, freeing one of my hands to take my change. "I've even put that can inside one of the others, so they'd know it was trash. And they still didn't take it." I pick up the change from the counter and slide it into my pocket. "I even put a sign on it. THIS IS TRASH. PLEASE THROW IT AWAY. Know what they did?" I shake my head and look over to where Micah is sitting, taking small bites from his ice cream, leaving tiny divots in it. Like a golf ball. "They took the sign and left the can."

Chloe

"Maybe write it directly on the can," I say, and I turn slightly to walk back over to the table, but she continues.

"I tried that," she says. "Wrote THIS IS TRASH right on the side of it with a Sharpie. Big black letters. Didn't work. It's as if they thought I was this senile old lady who needed reminding. Like I had little Post-its all over my house. THIS IS THE TELEVISION. THIS IS THE REFRIGERATOR." I smile at that one, thinking about a house filled with little reminders. It's funny and then suddenly it isn't because suddenly I'm thinking about notes not on things, but on people. *Sad. Quiet. Dark. Crazy.* I don't know what my label would say. All I can imagine is a tiny square of pink paper right on my chest, and it's blank.

"Want me to show you something?" I ask Micah as I walk toward him. He nods, and for the seventieth time this week, I am sure that he understands way more than he lets on. "Look," I say, lifting my cone so the pointy end is just over my mouth. I bite off the tip. "See?" I say, around a mouthful of melted ice cream. "Now you can just suck it through the hole." We sit in the back table of a shop in the middle of what feels like winter, eating ice cream. Eating it in reverse, upside down. Exactly backward.

People think that a mortuary is scary. I did, too, until my father decided he'd had enough of lobstering and painting houses and making wreaths and raking blueberries, trying to somehow gather enough money in as many ways as possible to make ends meet. It only took a year for him to get his funeral home license, since he doesn't actually prepare bodies. Nights and weekends he'd drive into Portland to take classes. Courses like anatomy and embalming and ethics and accounting. Courses in small business management and pathology and risk management. Three semesters and some continuing education credits every year and anyone can be a mortician. Although they don't like to be called that. They prefer "funeral service providers" or "mortuary science professionals." But it's all the same thing. All of them take care of dead people.

Shana's Goth friends think it's cool that our dad's a mortician. They sometimes hang around across the street, leaning against light posts and blowing smoke into rings over their heads. I think they're thinking *Addams Family* or *Beetlejuice*, but actually it's like having your father run just about any other small business, like a flower shop or a bakery or a shoe store. But I guess in my dad's business, there's a lot more crying. And that's the worst part. The crying. You can't get away from it. Women wiping red eyes as they pass you on the front steps. Men blowing their noses into handkerchiefs that they quickly stuff back into their pockets.

There's no one on the steps today. No cars in back, in the spaces marked RESERVED FOR PATRONS OF PARSON HILLS. Of course what I'm thinking is that the actual patrons are dead people and they don't really need parking places.

Chloe

Micah follows me up the back steps and through the door that directs "patrons" to the front entrance. When Micah first came to us, my parents tried to shield him from the mortuary, even using the outside entrance to our apartment upstairs. But eventually we had bigger things to worry about.

The back office is just what you'd expect: metal filing cabinets, a big wooden desk with a computer and a phone, and a blotter with business cards stuck under it.

"Hi, Dad," I say, dropping into one of the chairs facing his desk. My father holds up one finger, his other hand working across the number keys of his keyboard. And this is where the Goth kids' image of this place breaks down. My father, typing away at his computer, is wearing his SURF NAKED T-shirt, which he used to paint houses in, and a pair of old gray fleece pants. His glasses are perched on the end of his nose à la Santa Claus, because when he has to do close-up work, he can't see out of his regular glasses and he still refuses to get bifocals, saying he's way too young. He can dress like this on slow days because in this business there aren't any walk-ins. They always call ahead. A couple more clicks and he looks up.

"How was the playground?" he asks, looking from me to Micah. "And the ice cream," he says, smiling. "Let me guess." He mock-studies Micah for a minute, as if he's studying tea leaves in the bottom of a cup. "Chocolate?" he asks, and I laugh at Micah's surprise.

"Your mouth," I say, pointing to my own. Micah puts his hand to his lips, feeling the sticky residue of his ice-cream cone still ringing his mouth and giving him a very faint brown goatee.

"How was school?" my father asks, again looking briefly from Micah to me. He shrugs, then I shrug. "That good, huh?" He turns back to his computer screen, frowning.

"Upstairs?" Micah asks, unzipping his coat.

"I'll be up in a few minutes," my father says without looking back at either of us. Micah heads toward the stairs on the other side of the hallway. "I think Shana's in the chapel," Dad tells me. I get up and loosen my scarf from around my neck, letting it hang down either side of my chest and brush at my knees.

"Hey," I say, entering the chapel. She's running a Dust-Vac along the velvet cushion in the front pew, so I'm not sure if she's heard me or not. Shana's been spending more and more time down here helping out. Putting out new boxes of tissues in the foyer. Throwing away dead flower arrangements. Until lately, that was one of the things my father was really good at. He noticed the details. Like, he has a contract with the florist over on Nutmeg Avenue. Every Thursday they deliver two new arrangements, just in case the families forget. It happens a lot. No one forgets flowers at weddings, but flowers at funerals? People forget.

I watch Shana as she concentrates on the cushion, pushing the vacuum deep into the edges, where salt from kids' boots and bits of torn tissue can accumulate. Her hair is pulled back from her face in a low ponytail, and without all of her usual clown makeup, I can see how pretty she is. Sometimes it's hard for me to think of this Shana—my sister Shana—and that other Shana—the Goth, depressed Shana—as the same person. It's like she has an alter ego, but instead of running into a phone booth or into an alley to change, she does it right at home in her room. And if she is some superhero or even some supervillain, what's her super power? I mean, cynicism isn't really a power—or it's a pretty lame one. When I see those people she hangs out with, like the one with the purple bob and the green nose ring that I swear looks like a booger. Or the one with the really tall boots that buckle all the way up to his knees and make it hard for him to walk in the snow. Or the one with the leather trench coat that looks brown and not black at all. (I wonder if the other Goths make fun of him for that.) When I see all of them I keep wanting to say, "Shana, you're smarter than that. These people are pretending to be all deep and thoughtful, but you already are those things. Always have been. And the crap that you put on in front of the mirror every night just covers all of that up." But, of course, I don't. I just lie on her bed, watching as she plays dress up, and ask if I can come with her.

"What are you doing?" Shana asks, and I realize that the vacuum is quiet.

"Just hanging out," I say, looking around at the coffin

stand and the empty pews, still full of programs from the last funeral.

"Soaking in the atmosphere?" she asks, smiling at me.

"Well, it *is* restful."

"More like rest in peaceful," she says, making me laugh. She laughs, too, and for a minute it feels like it used to, but then we stop and the chapel goes quiet again. "Guess I better finish this," she says.

"Guess so." I turn and walk down the aisle and toward the stairs. Better check on Micah, I think. As I climb the steps upstairs, I realize I do the same thing as my father does. I check on everyone, too. Only I pay attention, and I do it in the daytime, making sure that everyone's okay. Or at least as okay as they can be. But there's one problem: If they weren't okay, I wouldn't know what to do.

Sometimes, after Shana leaves and Micah is quiet and my dad has settled into the studio, I listen to the radio. Not music, but talk radio. Mostly NPR, but if it's really late, I'll turn on this show called *Coast to Coast*. It's all about weird things, like alien abductions and crop circles and Bigfoot sightings and secret societies in ancient Egypt. Tonight the guest is some guy who thinks that organic foods are just a government ploy to get all of us to ingest some compound that will turn us all invisible. I've heard it before, so I turn it off. A while ago, they had this guy on, John something, from Fairbanks, Alaska. He's been building this ice wall for a couple of years now, adding to it constantly day after day. It melts down every summer, almost melting away. Then, once it's cold enough, he turns on the hose and pumps water over it, trying to make it freeze evenly enough to support its own weight. I was so interested in the story that I went to the Alpine Club website and read all about it. I even printed one of the photos and hung it over my desk. The thing was, as interested as I was in how big it got, how high it reached, and all that, I was way more interested in what he said at the end of the interview. When the host asked him why he did it, he paused for a minute. I turned the knob on my radio a bit to make sure I didn't miss it. *I like the idea of creating something out of something so ordinary—ice. I like that even in that, there's magic.*

CHAPTER FOUR

Shana

SOMETIMES AFTER BEING out at the clubs, I just want to shed all of the crap—the leather, the metal studs and safety pins, the smell of cigarettes, and the attitude. This morning I'm standing naked in front of my mirror, just looking at myself without all the black and white. Dad starts calling, in his business voice, wanting something, but I just ignore it. I turn to the side a little bit, stripes of sun from the venetian blinds falling across my stomach, creases on my face from the pillow. No, I'm not thrilled with what the mirror is showing me, like my hips are too bulgy and my breasts a little uneven, but at least it's *me*, just me, all pared down. I don't do this too much, because like pretty much everything else, it makes me think of my mom. Like when I first had my period, she got me to stand beside her at this same mirror, back when it was in the other house, both of us in our pajamas. She told me that nothing was more mysterious or beautiful than the human body, that women's bodies were the most beautiful of all. Yeah, I know, but she was painting a lot then, really looking at bodies, and also she was just like that. She believed in ordinary mysteries. She told me that people would die from lack of sleep sooner than from lack of food, that by the time you turn seventy, your heart will have beat over two billion times, that there are forty-five miles of nerves in the body, that when first conceived, every living human spent a half an hour as a single cell.

I sometimes wish I could become a single cell again, just undivide and undivide all these versions of myself until I'm left with something so simple. But it's a stupid wish, I know. Be a single cell, then divide once and your problems are doubled. That's how it is. Everyone now feels sorry for us, like we were raised by this crazy weirdo, so I never talk to anyone about this stuff, but if I did, I could tell them that right after that, after telling me we used to be a single cell, she whispered to me that it was probably a *hell* of a lot easier finding jeans that fit. And we both started laughing at the idea of it. Then the laughing became funnier than the idea, until we were laughing so hard that Chloe and Dad came running in to see what was going on. Nothing was wrong that day, and not two years later when she gave almost the same speech to Chloe after she got her period, and not even two years after that, when Micah first came to live with us. She would tell him things all the time; I would hear her talking to Micah in the kitchen or in her studio, when she didn't think any of us were around. I think she talked to him mostly because he couldn't understand anything she was saying. She could just talk. One day, when I was messing around with the watercolors she'd given me, and I had the radio tuned to a baseball game because I knew at dinner Dad would be asking me all the stats, I could hear her talking to Micah while she stretched and stapled more canvases, rattling off more facts while he played with his LEGOs. She told him that the human brain is 85 percent water, that the left lung is smaller than the right, to leave room for the heart. *Isn't that incredible, sweetheart?* I heard her say. There followed a long pause, her staple gun quiet, just the sound of the LEGOs spilling, and then, on the day my life started to end, I heard her tell him that there was an angel sitting on the rocking chair in the corner of the room, and that the angel's feet were bleeding.

When Dad calls me again, then knocks, I throw on a Rolling Stones T-shirt and shorts, and he says through the door that he needs to talk to me. It sounds like I'm busted, but I know he has heard me come in late before, and I always figured it was like we had this silent agreement—I do what I want, and he's too scattered to care. That works. He motions me down the hall, and I almost smile, thinking how much not like a mortician he always looks. Right now he's wearing old swim trunks with flames painted up the sides, and a hooded sweatshirt with an ad for Corona embossed on the front, a hula girl holding a ukulele and a beer bottle.

"Can I ask you a question?" he says, looking back over his shoulder as he walks down the hall ahead of me.

"You just did," I say.

"You know, those look like ordinary pants, but I guess they're really your smarty-pants, huh?" It's an old joke of his, as old as I can remember, but it still makes me smile despite myself.

"Dad, what is this about?"

"You'll see."

We pass Chloe in her room, where she's lining up the jars of sea glass on her windowsill, turning them this way and that, the way she always does, so that the morning sun will shine through them in colored patterns on her wall. It's like she lives inside a giant kaleidoscope. I think it's sad, in a way, that if you live in a kaleidoscope you have to do your own turning. Someone ought to do the turning for you. And something about what she's doing bugs me, too . . . more than bugs me, like last week with the red sea glass. I get really pissed, like I almost want to hit her, and I don't know why. I see her creeping around the corners of grocery stores, or playing with the glass jars, or plucking the same string over and over on Dad's guitar, and I think, *Why can't you just be normal?* But, you know, Welcome to Irony World, because I'm usually thinking this after I've Goth'd out my face, or cut my hair with a steak knife, maybe, or made plans to meet a guy friend of mine who shaves off his eyebrows and talks about piercing his penis.

We reach the kitchen, and Dad finally turns around to face me. Micah is on the floor, eating sugar out of the bowl with a spoon. He does this about twice a day, and we are all supposed to watch out for it, but usually Dad forgets to. Apparently, an occasional piece of candy was the only good thing about life in Russia. "*Dad*," I say, then turn back around to Micah. "*Nyet sakharńjj*," I tell him in the little bit of Russian I have learned. "No sugar." Micah looks up at me, his mouth ringed white like a powdered doughnut, his tiny eyes black and guarded. He stares at me, and I think he must assume that he has three sisters—me, Chloe, and the freaky chick in the black and white. The very first time I came out of my bedroom dressed in Goth, he was sitting in the hallway playing with wadded-up balls of aluminum foil. He stared at me for a full five seconds before his mouth dropped into a flattened oval and his face reddened, and for a second I thought he couldn't breathe until the crying came out of him all at once. The screaming and the crying, in one sudden burst, and getting down next to him only made it worse, and all I could do was shush him and call for Chloe and Dad. The whole time Micah kept screaming something in Russian, some word that sounded like "*pray scratch knee, pray scratch knee*," over and over. The next day it took us an hour with the phonetic dictionary to figure out what he meant. I let Chloe do the looking up—the smart one, good with dictionaries. She kept thumbing back and forth, asking me over and over what I thought I had heard him say, and when she was about to give up she stopped, put her finger in the middle of the page, and said, "Here it is. *Ghost*," she said quietly. "He thinks you're a ghost."

Dad stops next to the pantry and slaps his palm against the door down to the mortuary. "The thing is, I want to offer you a job," he says. "I want you to work for me."

"And you couldn't tell me this in other parts of the house?"

"No. I want you to say yes, and we'll get you started." I have a strong feeling that this has to do with the six-month visit from the social worker, which is supposed to happen in three weeks. This is one of the biggies, an "official visit," as they call it, like we are the First Family hosting a dignitary. But there's nothing dignified about it—they walk all around with clipboards, writing down our whole lives. I wonder how much better it might look to have at least one daughter, the "bad" one, all cleaned up and responsible. Really, you can't blame Dad.

Micah sits on the floor, sliding his foot back and forth across the linoleum. I wonder if he still sees me as a ghost, or as a reverse ghost, someone who sometimes comes back into her body. I think about Mom again, telling us all the time that the body is 80 percent water, like it was some kind of miracle. I wonder if she understood—if we are that much water, how easy is it for us to just one day evaporate?

A job. It sounds so normal, so vanilla, so regular life, even if it is in the mortuary. I look at my dad. "Okay," I tell him.

Hardly anyone believes it, but the funeral business has off times, just like any other business. July is slow (right after Christmas is the busiest). Fall is steady, but not great. This month is one of the worst, and we sometimes go days without a service. This is also the time they have this conference for mortuary owners and technicians, where they go to Florida and learn new embalming methods and play golf. Dad never goes, but he sends the two guys who work for us doing all the body prep work. They work for us and three other mortuaries in town, journeymen, like they are first basemen instead of embalmers. It's just cheaper that way. Or cost-effective, I guess I should say, now that I'm in the biz.

I find out I will be "working with" Mr. Tucker, who tells me to call him Vernon, like I haven't been doing that already anyway. Dad is so bossy-boss it makes me laugh. He tells me he is glad to "have me aboard" and that "his door is always open." I tell him no, sometimes I close it because he snores. He leaves me to Vernon, this retired guy who's been working here almost four years now, who used to sell car stereos at Radio Shack. Now Vernon does a little bit of everything, except the technical work (the journeymen) and meeting with clients (Dad does that). He orders the supplies and plays the organ if people want that (most don't these days—too cliché, I think), and makes sure the heating oil is delivered, and oils the hinges on doors, and dusts, and . . . just everything. He will even fill in as a pallbearer if they are short one, and he cries, really cries, at every service, like he knew the person and his heart is broken. For services he wears this gray suit that is too short for him, and this old red-and-blue-striped tie, and—this could almost make me fall in love with him—a little white square of handkerchief, sticking out of the pocket. He is about the sweetest guy I ever met.

"Now, I always think it's good to look busy, even if you aren't," he says, reaching into a box of cleaning supplies in the chapel closet.

"In general, or just at work?"

He smiles with teeth so even that they must be dentures. His white hair is patted neatly in place, the collar of his plaid shirt buttoned all the way up. "At home, I don't worry about it too much." He hands me a feather duster, keeping an identical one for himself.

"His and hers," I say. We go after the pews and the podium and the organ and the potted plants. First dust, then vacuum, he tells me, always.

"Let me ask you," he says, still dusting, "you know how your 7-Eleven, your Stop & Shop, your—"

"Convenience stores," I say.

He points his duster at me, the feathers moving. "Exactly."

"What about them?"

"Well, they are all open all the time, around the clock, all night, even on Christmas and New Year's, am I right?"

"Yeah . . ."

He stops and looks at me. "So how come they have locks on the doors? Big dead bolts? Serious locks, I'm talking."

I laugh. "So these are the deep thoughts you think, while you're down here facing mortality every day?"

He shrugs, scratches his chin. "Somebody has to."

"Got any more?" He trades the dusters for rags and lemon polish, and we tackle the pews.

"Oh, sure. The guys who drive the snowplows . . . how do they get to work?"

I laugh again, my hair swinging down into my vision as I polish the wood. "More?"

"Naw, don't want to make your head explode on the very first day. I will ask, though, how your mother is doing. Pete just gives me the same answer every time."

I stiffen up, the smell of the lemon polish suddenly close to making me throw up. I swallow. "She's fine," I say, as quickly as I can.

"*That's* the answer. Must be genetic inclination to give it."

I see him blushing above his shirt collar, his neck darkening, and for half a second I wish I could be better about it, just tell him how she *really* is. For that half second, I feel sorry for him, in a way I can't explain. We continue along in silence, the pews shining under the banks of track lights.

"We can knock off for the day, or you can," he says. "You know, Shana, keep an eye on your dad, will you?"

I look at him. "What do you mean?"

"I mean this is a good business. He's a good man. Just keep an eye on him."

I shrug. "Okay."

"One more thing," he says, and I feel myself stiffen up again. "How come the word *phonetic* isn't spelled the way it sounds?"

For some reason, after just the first two hours of work, I'm feeling better than I have in a long time. Even with this question about Mom, I know Vernon didn't mean it the way other people usually do. When they say, *How's your mother?*, what they really mean is something like, *Any dead bodies at the accident scene?* That's just how people are, why they are so easy to hate. That's what my friend Jason says, the guy who wants to pierce his penis—*it's just so easy, go to a mall, go into Gap, hate all you see.* Sometimes, I don't want to think he's right.

Chloe sits on my bed while I put on makeup, watching me, the same way I used to watch Mom putting on mascara and lip gloss when she and Dad had a party or a gallery show to go to. I'm already thinking that tomorrow after school I will get into the back room, where Dad keeps his records, and start straightening things up a little bit. That place is a mess, even Vernon said so. Actually, he said, "Our feather dusters and Pledge are helpless against it." Total oddball, but you have to love him.

"Are you going to the Bat Club?" Chloe asks.

"Sunday night, Chlo. They're all closed."

She takes the VISIT NIAGARA FALLS pillow from my bed, throws it into the air, then ducks to one side just before it hits her on the head. I used to play the same game, pretending that the pillow was a boulder or a dagger, that I was brave and smart enough to get out of harm's way.

"Where, then?"

I shrug. "We just hang out in Old Port, on the wharf. We watch crap float in the water, try to throw cigarette butts into the Styrofoam cups."

"You smoke?"

"No. I have, but I don't."

"Is it fun?" She throws the pillow again, ducks away. I smile, thinking somehow that Vernon would probably like this game, and have a lot to say about Niagara Falls as well. Really, this was my best day in a long time. I catch Chlo's eye in the mirror.

"Is what fun, throwing cigs? Yeah, it's a riot."

"No. Old Port, hanging out. Is it fun?"

I shrug again. "Something to do, I guess."

"Take me with you."

I look at her again, just as she throws the pillow. She catches my eye and forgets to duck out of the way, so that the pillow hits her on the side of the face. Chlo looks away, anticipating my usual answer.

"Sure," I tell her instead, and she looks up. "You can come."

CHAPTER FIVE

Chloe

"IT MUST BE really creepy living above all those dead people," Blaine says, flipping his cigarette butt into the street, where it makes a soft sizzle as it hits the ice.

"I guess," I say, trying not to look directly at him. Every time I do, I have to bite the inside of my cheek to keep from laughing, and I wonder how they do it, how they can look at each other and have conversations without just busting up. Other than the fact that Blaine has a *fake* eyebrow ring and a *fake* ring through his nose, like he thinks he's Ferdinand the Bull or something, he has lipstick on his teeth. Like my grandmother used to get sometimes if she smiled too much after putting it on. I keep touching my mouth, wondering if he will get the point that something's wrong, but he doesn't.

"It's cool that your father is a mortician," he says, reaching into his coat pocket, dark brown, not black, and taking out another cigarette.

"I don't think about it much," I say. "Though it is kind of weird when he brings his work home with him." Blaine doesn't laugh. I shoot a look over at Shana, who is pressed up against Jason, but she doesn't look back. The four of us are huddled into the doorway of a kitchen supply shop, waiting for the others. Like a poster for a terrible B movie—*Double Date of the Dead.* People keep walking by in twos and fours, heading toward the pub at the end of the block or the seafood restaurant out on the dock. As a couple walks past us holding hands, the woman looks over at where we're sitting and half smiles at me. I smile back, forgetting the first rule of Gothdom: *Never smile.* Blaine scowls at them, making her smile more. She tilts her head slightly as she looks at me again, making me think of the old *Sesame Street* song, "One of these things is not like the others . . . one of these things just doesn't belong. . . ."

I asked Shana what I should wear after she told me I could come.

"Anything warm," she said, pulling her heavy black wool tights out of her dresser drawer. Top three drawers, regular clothes. Bottom drawer, Goth crap. I turned to head across the living room to my bedroom to change but stopped when I heard her whisper my name. "Chloe," she hissed across the darkness. "Nothing pink."

Duh, I said to myself, pulling out a drawer on my dresser.

It's the same four-drawer dresser as Shana's, only in mine the bottom drawer isn't filled with studded leather dog collars and handcuff bracelets and T-shirts that look like you just barely survived a shark attack. My bottom drawer is filled with something a lot more frightening. My bottom drawer is filled with my mother's paintings, the ones she did last fall.

The best I could do was my dark blue fleece jacket over navy cords, a T-shirt, and a wool sweater.

"Don't you have another hat?" Shana asked as I came out of my room, zipping up my coat.

"You know I don't," I said, sitting on the floor to lace up my boots. Shana sighed and walked back into her room, emerging with her gray wool ski hat with the tiny pocket on the front.

"In case I need to store something?" I asked, taking the hat from her and switching it out for mine.

"It's just that your hat is so. . . ."

"Cool?" I asked, fingering the tiny multicolored pompoms that are stitched all over the top of it.

"I was thinking of another word," Shana said, pulling at her own boots.

"*Awesome?*" I asked.

"Not quite." We both stepped out into the hallway.

"*Breathtaking?*"

Shana pulled the door closed with a soft click. "No, not that," she said, heading toward the front stairs.

Chloe

"*Amazing*?" I asked, stretching out the *a*'s. She shook her head at me before turning to walk down the stairs. We moved along in silence after that, down the back steps, past the lit window where I could see Vernon and Micah hunched over another one of their marathon Monopoly games. You always have to watch Vernon because he cheats. Micah mostly just plays with the little car. I follow Shana down the sidewalk and along Exchange Street toward the water. Even though it was freezing cold, our breath coming out in little puffs in front of us, I couldn't help feeling a little warm. Before she turned away from me, I saw it. Even with all the makeup on, I saw a glimmer of my sister, just for an instant, but long enough for me to know that she is still in there, underneath everything.

"So, get this," Sammy says, leaning against the bricks on the side of the grocery store. Once the other three arrived, the ones we were apparently waiting for, we all shuffled down to the market to pick up more clove cigarettes. *Shuffled* is the key word, because Goths don't walk. They amble. They clomp. They stride when need be, but they do not walk.

"Wait," Jason says, coming out of the store and pulling back on his gloves. "Start over."

"So, I'm sitting there, waiting for Mom to come in—"

"He got caught coming in late," says Blaine, leaning close enough to me that I can smell his Polo. Black lipstick and cologne. Weird.

"And instead of reading me the riot act or telling me I'm grounded for life, she tells me she understands this phase I'm going through. She tells me that when she was my age, she used to sneak out to meet her friends, too. She tells me she *empathizes*."

"Man, that's the worst," says a girl who told me her name was Magenta. I thought, *Like on* Blue's Clues? "I hate it when they try to bond with you. Like they understand half of the shit we have to deal with." I squint across the group at Shana, but she just shakes her head.

"So Chloe," Magenta says. She flips her hair (which is, of course, magenta) out of her eyes. "What's your story?"

"My story." I look over at Shana, but she doesn't say anything. And this is where it gets tricky. It's not like anyone in my family has ever said that anything's off limits or a secret, but it's kind of understood. I don't know how much Shana's told them. Has she told them about Micah, how he has a sweet tooth and is afraid of the dark and cries himself to sleep almost every night? Or about how Dad talks to himself and won't eat and chain-smokes on the roof for hours every time he gets home from the hospital? Or how once when we got home from school, our mom had cut her wrist on purpose because she said an angel told her to?

"She's an artist," Shana says. For a second, I think she means our mom, but then I realize she's talking about me. I look at her, but she's staring out at the water across the street.

"Cool," Magenta says, and I know what she's thinking. Tortured. Moody. Angst ridden. Everyone is quiet for a couple of minutes as a fishing boat slips past, the noise of its motor blown away from us in the wind.

"I'm cold," Sammy says, rubbing his gloved hands up and down his arms.

"Coffee?" Jason asks. Nods all around. We walk along the far sidewalk. The one built on top of the seawall. The waves slap against the dock pilings, pulling at the barnacles that cling to them. When we were little, my mother told us a story about barnacles, about how they were once magical creatures, capable of making any wish come true. But one day, wooed by greed and power, the barnacles decided to serve the Dark Sea King. They joined him in a battle against the merpeople, where they used their magic to bring terrible pain and suffering to the other creatures in the ocean. Finally defeated, the Dark Sea King and all of his followers were banished by the other kings and queens. They decided that the fate for the barnacles should be that they would have to live at the whim of the ocean tides. Always wanting, never satisfied.

I'm imagining a dark, old coffee shop at the end of one of the alleyways, with wooden spools for tables and lights that flicker whenever the wind blows too hard. The coffee shop is actually a Starbucks.

"Six grande coffees," Jason says to the girl behind the counter. "Black."

"Black. Of course," she says, raising her eyebrow at me. I guess being the only one not in clown makeup somehow makes me her ally. She can't be more than a couple years older than the rest of them.

"Hold the cream," Sammy says. "And the sarcasm."

"Why don't you guys find a table?" Shana says, actually making a shooing motion with her hand. "Chloe and I'll get the coffees." We stand, watching the girl behind the counter slowly fill cups with the house blend. "They can be such children sometimes."

"Sometimes?" I ask, but the way she cuts her eyes at me tells me to stop the comments. The girl puts four cups on the counter in front of us and turns to finish the other two.

"You got it?" Shana asks, lifting her chin toward the back of the girl's head. I nod as she picks up two cups in each hand and carries them over to the group now huddled in the back, making a mother sitting with her toddler nervous.

"Go ahead, I won't tell," the girl says, nodding at the container of cream sitting at the edge of the counter. "I'm thinking you don't like your coffee like you like your friends."

"Dark and surly?" I ask, making her smile.

"How about acidic and childish?"

"They're not really my friends," I say, feeling guilty for a moment, like I'm abandoning Shana.

"They could be mine," she says. "I could totally fit into

the whole Goth thing." I tilt my head at her. "My name's Raven." She sees the look on my face and laughs. "Really. It is."

"You could *totally* be Goth with a name like that," I say, pouring some cream into my coffee and watching it spin in a slow, lazy circle.

"Yeah, my name and a lobotomy maybe," she says. "Wait." She turns and pulls another cup off the counter behind her. "Watch this." She plunges the steamer tip into a pitcher of milk, making it hiss for a moment. Then slowly she pours the milk into the coffee, careful to let it slide across the top. She twists her wrist, moving the last drizzle of milk across the tan surface. "Look." There on the surface of the frothy milk she has made a star.

"Wow," I say, afraid to breathe too hard for fear of messing it up. I jump when someone touches my shoulder.

"Chloe, are you coming?" Shana asks, picking up her cup. The one without the cream.

"See you around," Raven says. She turns and walks toward the other end of the counter.

"What was that all about?" Shana asks. I shrug and take a sip from my coffee. "She was weird." I take another sip of my coffee to keep from laughing. Of course. The kids dressing all in black because they think death is cool and pain is deep are normal. The barista who can make art with milk is weird.

I sit through a conversation about which bug is the grossest (the puss moth caterpillar), which artist is the most tortured (tie between Sylvia Plath and Virginia Woolf), and which band is the darkest (no agreement could be reached) before Shana finally announces that it's time to head home. I stand off to the side while she says good night to Jason. They stand close to each other under the glowing green neon of the Starbucks sign. He puts his hand on her shoulder before turning and heading down Canal Street. I guess Goths don't kiss.

We sit on the floor of the landing outside our front door and slide off our boots. "Why did you tell them I'm an artist?" I ask, slipping off my wool socks, damp from the slush.

"Because you are," Shana says, looking up at me.

"Not anymore."

"I don't think you're an artist because you paint or you draw or you play music." She pushes herself to standing and eases the front door open, dropping her voice to a whisper. "I think if you're an artist, it's because you're born to be one." We hang our coats up on the hooks near the door, and take off our boots, letting the slush slowly melt into puddles on the floor. I walk down the hall and peer into Micah's room. He's asleep, his outer space sheets twisted around his legs. I go in and try to untangle him, feeling Shana watching me from the doorway. Micah rolls over and mumbles something. I put my hand on his head, willing him back to sleep.

"Chlo-ee," he mumbles.

Chloe

"I better go," Shana says from behind me. "If he wakes up and sees me like this, he'll freak." Shana turns to walk toward her bedroom.

"Shana?" I whisper, but she doesn't turn around. I bend and lay a hand on Micah's shoulder. He's so warm underneath his flannel pajamas with cartoon lizards crawling all over them.

"Chlo-ee," Micah says again. "Carry me."

"Okay," I say smiling, "but you'll have to help me." At three, when he first came to live with us, I could lift him, but now just one year later and I can't pick him up from standing, much less when he's lying down half asleep.

He stirs slightly under my hand, murmuring again. "Chlo-ee. Carry."

I manage to help him stand, bundling some of the blankets from his bed under my arm. He'd rather sleep on the floor in my room than in his own bed. I lead him down the hall and push the door open with my hip. I help him sit on the edge of my bed while I make a nest for him on my floor. I get him comfortable and pull the comforter from my bed to tuck around him.

"Chlo-ee?" he says again.

"Shh. Go back to sleep," I say. "It's late." I brush his dark hair away from his cheek, letting my hand rest on his head until his breathing deepens. I walk out into the hall and pull a couple of our camp blankets out of the linen closet, hearing the faint tinkle of sand on the wood floor as each one falls open. We haven't used these since we left Brunswick. I walk back into my room, feeling the grit of sand under my bare feet. I don't bother to get into my pajamas, sliding into bed in my cords and T-shirt and pulling the blankets up to my chin.

I wonder if that's right. That you're born as an artist, able to take things from your mind and put them on canvas or find them in a block of wood or create them out of bits of glass and yarn and pieces of torn paper. My mother is a painter, an almost famous one. She doesn't paint lighthouses or blueberry barrens or lobster boats. She's a portrait artist, but her paintings are like nothing anyone's ever seen before. Two years ago, a writer from the *New York Times* came to our house and talked to her about her work, following her all over our property. To the barn to see her studio. To the beach where she'd walk every morning. To the garden to see her tomatoes. A week later a photographer came out and took pictures of her, painting, walking, sitting. She was named an "Artist You Need to Know" by the *Times*. After that, her paintings were everywhere. Huge faces of blue and green and red. The *Times* called her "soulful." A gallery owner in SoHo called her "provocative."

I used to stand in the doorway of her studio, watching her. She would stare at the blank canvas for sometimes an hour or more, silent, barely breathing. I found myself slowing my breathing to match hers, finding the same rhythm. The same pulse. It was the way she put the color to the canvas that seemed to captivate everyone. The bold streaks of primary colors, applied first with a spatula. The paint sometimes running off the canvas in rivers, spilling onto the wooden floor of her studio. Once she started a painting it was hard for her to stop; she often worked far into the night. Sometimes she would paint from photographs. Or people would come to her studio to pose for her. After the *Times* article, she couldn't keep up with the demand. Her garden grew over with weeds. Her walks on the beach all but disappeared. She painted until her hands ached, until her eyes grew tired. *You're just overworked* my father told her when she started complaining of headaches. *You need to rest* he told her when she said sometimes the sunlight seemed too bright. When we moved to the city, the bad stuff followed us, like a stray who refused to go back home. Amazingly her work didn't suffer. Each painting seemed better than the last. Of course that was before. She still paints, but it's different now.

Micah mumbles again in his sleep, and I sit up slightly to look at him over the edge of the bed. He is curled tightly, one arm covering his face. I lean back against my pillow, feeling the scratch of sand against my cheek as I turn on my side. Outside my window is a streetlight, with that white halo of light all around it. I always slip down in my bed so I can line up the halo with the jars of sea glass, watch the colors wink in the faint light, a tiny red ship on a sea of greens and blues. I stare through the jars, past them, trying to see the night sky. Then the colors seem to shift against one another, the light moving. I close my eyes, willing it to stop. I don't want to see things from the inside like my mother, inside the light or inside a painting, my dreams spilling into my waking life. As much as I love my mother, even admire her in ways, I know one thing for sure—I don't want to become her. I open my eyes again and watch the light still shifting, still moving. It isn't until I ignore the jars and see beyond them into the night that I realize what is happening. I'm not imagining things. The light *is* moving, bouncing in the night. Sometime, while I was lying here watching but not seeing, it started to snow.

Chloe

CHAPTER SIX

Shana

THE LONGER I work here, the more I find out there is to do. I also figure out that Vernon Tucker is like one of those secretaries in a big company. The kind that if she quit, the whole place would fall apart and the bosses would be lost. It's only ten o'clock in the morning and already he has cleaned the prep room with disinfectant, ordered a new monoseal casket and three cremation caskets for the showroom, driven to Sam's Club for paper towels and sponges, and arranged for Terry's Auto to come out and look at our hearse because the engine keeps knocking going uphill. Once it broke down on the way to a burial, with a casket in the back, and Vernon had to go into a Chuck E. Cheese to call for help while Dad tried to console the mourners. Vernon walked out with a *THE PLACE FOR FUN!* stamp on the back of his hand, and we had to tow the hearse to the burial site. Dad said it was the worst day of his life, though by now I imagine it's like number thirty on that list. In fact, he's going to visit her at the hospital today, so by tonight it will be number thirty-one. And I get to have a stomach-ache all day.

And as if that weren't enough, for two days now, since I took Chloe down to the wharf, she will barely talk to me. Not that I'm the most talkative one either, but like yester-day we were headed down the hall to the kitchen for the pizza Dad ordered, and I said, "Slow walking contest!" and started taking steps that were maybe an inch long. It's something we've done since we were really little kids, and the winner would always be the one with the most patience, who could tolerate taking a quarter-inch step every minute or so, to the point where it would take a half hour to walk three feet. The only rule was you had to convey a sense of movement, though that's not how we phrased it when we were five and six; we just said, *no real stopping*. We'd laugh so hard because of how ridiculous it looked, the two of us almost like statues in the middle of the mall, one or the other occasionally shouting, "I'm winning!" We'd play until someone quit, but yesterday Chloe didn't even try, she just kept walking normally down the hall. And I didn't quit be-cause, I don't know, it felt stupider to quit, but not by much. By the time I got to the kitchen Chloe was on her second slice, standing over the sink to eat it. "Looks like you won," she said, not even looking at me.

Vernon likes me, which means he talks to me. He gets all

his news from tabloids, because he doesn't trust the media, he says. I don't have the heart to point out that tabloids are media, too. Right now we're in the showroom, as he calls it, cleaning all the caskets. We have to vacuum all the satin, really clean it, and dust the outside and then polish all the copper and bronze with this stuff meant for polishing pots and pans.

"Hey, young lady," he says. He calls me that, apparently never having seen me all Goth'd out. "Let me ask you. Do you think it's possible that Marilyn's ghost warned John Kennedy about his murder, but he refused to listen?"

I have no idea, really, who he's talking about. I mean, I know about Kennedy from school, but the rest . . . he might as well be talking about the Middle Ages. "I don't know," I say. "I think if ghosts could warn us about stuff, that's all we'd be listening to, all day."

He nods, pushing his polishing cloth in tiny circles around the copper. "Pretty smart," he says. I hear Dad upstairs, clomping around the kitchen in his good shoes. Vernon straightens up and wipes his face with his polishing cloth, which he always does. And then he is looking at my shirt and I feel creeped out for half a second that he's looking at my breasts. I get a lot of that from guys, because I'm kind of ahead of the development curve. At least I got a lot of it before I went Goth. But Vernon is just reading my latest T-shirt, which I keep making and then forgetting I'm wearing. I started making them the first day I got the job, just some old babydoll T's and a Sharpie and some cool writing. I keep making up pretend slogans for the business and suggesting them to Dad, who laughs a little bit and tells me to never, ever let a client see me wearing one. The first one I made said PARSON HILLS MORTUARY: WE PUT THE FUN IN FUNERAL! and I wrote FUN with little stars and confetti and champagne glasses around it. Chloe is the artist, but I can still draw pretty well. The next one said, ALL MEN ARE CREMATED EQUAL, with a drawing of the flag. Today's shirt says, YOUR UNDERTAKER—THE LAST PERSON TO EVER LET YOU DOWN. I showed a T-shirt to Jason one night, when nobody else showed up at Starbucks, and it was the weirdest thing. He laughed. I had never seen it before, not even a smile, and it surprised me so much I felt myself smiling, too. And it was hard to tell with all the makeup, but it looked like a really nice smile he had, not Hollywood nice, just real, like his eyes were smiling, too, the lines around them making little cracks in the white powder.

Twenty minutes later I hear Dad walking down the stairs, and my stomach knots up. Vernon and I are polishing the wooden caskets, which no one ever buys anyway because it's Dad's job to talk people into the more expensive ones. The good ones cost as much as ten thousand dollars. Dad steps down and stands there with his hands in his pockets, watching us, and the smell of his cologne cuts through the smell of the polish, making it to us before he does. The thing is, for his visits to the hospital to see her, he always wears one of his best suits, one of his dark ties, and it's cool that he wants to look nice, but it's the same suit he wears for services, when we have a funeral. I don't think he even makes the connection. I pointed that out to Chloe one time, and she got mad. "So what, Shana? Maybe he's just romantic. He just dresses up like it's a date." She hasn't been there yet. She doesn't know how it is. But I see him in that suit, and I always wonder if it's his way of letting himself think she is already dead. Or maybe wishing that she was.

"Looking good," he says, not actually looking at the caskets. He jingles the keys in his pocket. His eyes look almost yellow, the way mine do when I put on the white powder, so white my eyes can't compete. He will drive away in his car and be gone all day. When he comes back, he's like this total cliché—a pint of bourbon in a paper bag, a pack of cigarettes, which he normally never smokes, and his eyes all bloodshot, his suit wrinkled, his tie crooked. He looks like some ruined businessman, about to take the leap from the bridge, and I want to ask him sometimes if he can't be a little more original. But I never have time. He will get home and toss his keys on the hall table, and then he'll climb out one of our living room windows to the roof of the building that juts up next to ours, and sit out there half the night in a lawn chair, smoking and drinking. One corner of the roof is like this dandelion field of cigarette butts. He does that every time he comes home from a visit, and honestly I'm glad for it, because part of me worries that one of these days he just won't come home at all.

I ask Vernon for a break, and he says sure, break a leg, which hits him as really funny. I go upstairs and find Chloe in her room, playing with the jars of sea glass again. Actually, she is organizing more than playing, I guess, all the blues in one jar, yellows in another, greens in another. Then there's a jar with that single piece of red glass in it, all by itself. I also notice that she has been looking at Mom's paintings again. Her bottom drawer is open, and one painting is leaning against the wall. It's the worst one, from right near the end, showing this dark alleyway, a tunnel of red brick, the only light coming from an angel at the far end, crucified on a chain-link fence and bleeding, all the color drained from her face. I can't look at it, and don't need to . . . I will never get the picture out of my head.

"You shouldn't look at that," I tell her.

She shrugs, turning one of her jars. "If you think about it just as a painting, it's really beautiful."

"You don't think that. Besides, who in this house can look at it just as a painting?" My fingers lazily play with the ears of the stuffed dog that sits on her bed. I can't remember his name now.

"Don't tell me what I think," Chloe whispers.

I sit on the edge of her bed. Her back is still turned to me. "Okay, Chlo—*what* is your problem?"

She turns and looks at me, her face so flat it startles me. "I don't want you to tell anyone that I'm an artist. Ever."

"Fine. I'll just say that you like to paint, and you always carry around a sketch pad, and you have filled up about twenty other sketch pads, and you asked for pencils for your birthday, but I won't say you're an artist, ever. Okay?"

She shakes her head. "Go ahead and lie, then, because I don't do any of that, anymore. Ever."

"Yeah, right."

"Just leave, okay?" She takes the stuffed dog from me and tosses it on top of her pillow.

I nod. "Hey . . . where's Micah? Playing?"

"Yeah. Dad left him in the living room watching *Sponge-Bob* and eating a bag of M&M's. It's like kid paradise."

"Right. Nice, Dad. Babysitting basics—candy and cartoons."

Chloe turns away from me again, and I watch her rearrange the jars on her windowsill, moving them around, like a magician who's going to make the ball disappear underneath.

"Hey, so," I say. "What did you think of the other night?"

She turns, shrugs. "Raven was nice."

"Who?"

"The girl at the Starbucks. And why didn't you kiss Jason? Don't you kiss?"

My turn to shrug. I can hear SpongeBob from down the

hall, laughing and laughing. "I don't know," I tell her. "We aren't at that stage of our relationship." I say that because it's the kind of thing I hear people say on TV. Actually I am dying to kiss him, especially since I saw him smile. But I can't make myself, not even in my head, not through the makeup. I want to kiss *him*, not kiss whatever it is he's hiding behind. It would be like kissing through cellophane.

"Which is code for 'he's gross,' right?"

"Just stop it, Chloe, okay?"

"Dad left," she says.

"I know. He'll be back."

"Well, duh. I want to go next time." Which she says every time, but only because she has never been there. I have. Dad decided she was too young for the hospital. In some ways I think she might always be too young. Chloe watches me and clasps her hands together and turns them inside out so the knuckles crack, a habit of hers.

"Did you have fun the other night?" I ask her, trying to change the subject.

"Yeah. It was like *Dawn of the Dead*. You know, if the zombies were bland and stupid."

I shake my head. "God, you can be a bitch sometimes, Chlo. So I'm bland and stupid?"

"No, you aren't." She looks at me suddenly, almost like she might cry.

"Listen," I say, "give them another chance. I mean, they bore me sometimes, too, but at least they're nice, you know? I tell you what, Chlo, I kinda like a little boring these days."

"Yeah. But I don't know. . . ."

"I'll make you up."

"I'm real, Shana. You don't have to make me up."

I reach and pinch her nose, an old gesture I haven't done in forever. "We are so very, very funny today, aren't we?" I say, in my best British accent.

"Would you really? Make me up?"

"Better than Halloween. Full face, dog collar, trench coat. The most wicked fourteen-year-old in Portland."

"It is like Halloween, isn't it?" She thinks for a minute. "Okay. I'd like that. Promise I won't scare myself?"

My "break" ends up lasting like an hour, but Vernon never seems to mind. I keep checking the clock in the office, thinking Dad is almost there, Dad is pulling into the parking lot, Dad is getting out of the car. And I'm thinking I should be watching the calendar, too, because we have about a week before the social worker Nazis come around for their official visit, and Dad wants this place to be perfect. Already, since everything happened with Mom, our status is "conditional," whatever that means. We go to work in the office, filing some of the stacks of papers that Dad has been throwing into cardboard boxes and paper sacks.

"All this mess started maybe four months ago," Vernon says. "He barely bothers with the paperwork now, and you know, young lady, we are kind of like the police in that way."

"You like to bust heads?"

He smirks. "We are mostly paperwork."

I nod, and soon enough we fall into the rhythm of work, filing, sorting, making stacks in the middle of the floor. After a while I just show something to Vernon, and he either shakes his head or nods, meaning I either toss it or file it.

"Let me ask you something, since you're smart," Vernon says. He sits on the floor with his legs splayed, papers in little piles around him.

"Okay."

"Do you suppose it's possible that an ancient space-alien Aztec formula for tea made from aloe vera could really prolong life by up to forty years?"

"Let me guess, you read that somewhere. Or did the question just pop into your head?"

He smiles and looks up at me. "I'm seventy-three," he says, and I wait for him to make his point, then realize that *is* his point. He's scared to die. For a minute I can hardly breathe, not because I'm also afraid he will die, or afraid for him, but because of what I see in his face—the fear never goes away. I can live another sixty years or more and this feeling I have now will never end. I wonder if that can be true. Or maybe it's just Vernon, and everyone else finally figures things out enough not to feel afraid anymore. If someone said to me, *Explain this whole Goth thing*, that would be my answer. Everyone is afraid, and maybe if you put it on your face, wear it in your clothes, then you don't have to feel it inside. Or it lets you hide. That's what I wanted to tell Chloe and couldn't—just wait, people refuse to look your way, it's like you're invisible. I remember the first nights we lived in this building, how scared I was. And even though I'm always playing it off like I just live above a hospital or some clinic, the first night I knew there was a body downstairs in the prep room, I couldn't sleep, and stayed awake all night just looking at the ceiling, watching the pattern the light of my bedside table lamp made on the stamped tin, listening for footsteps coming up from the basement, afraid to breathe. I just want things to be how they seem. I want dead people to be dead. I don't want part of them to live on. I want to have a mother again who paints and bakes and takes me to soccer practice. I want a father who doesn't deal in dead bodies. I want people not to believe in ancient Aztec formulas or aliens or Marilyn's ghost. I want a sister who can paint and draw and it means only that—not that she is like my mother, slowly losing her mind to what I've always thought of as cancer of the imagination. I want everything to stay the same, and I want to look like me again, to take all the kohl eyeliner I own and flush it down the toilet.

"Vernon?" I say, and he looks up from his work. "You know, I think you are going to live twenty-five more years. Screw the Aztecs."

He grins. "That could almost be a T-shirt," he says. And I laugh.

And then I hear the door to the basement from the kitchen, and for a second I think that Dad is already back. But that's impossible. No, it's Chloe, calling my name.

"What?" I say, walking out of the office and around the corner. When I look up the stairs, her face is blank, stricken.

"Chlo? What's wrong?"

She shakes her head. "The TV's on, I thought he was in there. . . ."

"Chloe, what are you talking about?"

"Micah. He's not there. He's gone."

CHAPTER SEVEN

Chloe

IT'S NOT LIKE Micah's never disappeared before, and I guess in part that's why the adoption agency set our status as "conditional." If they had to give us a grade, I guess it would be a D–. Our family isn't quite failing, but close. Shana pulls on her coat and boots to go check his usual places. The toy store down the street and the bakery on the corner where the woman always gives him free cookies. Vernon tells us that as soon as the last appointment leaves, he'll help us. The thing is, we can't afford to screw up now—not in any way—or else we are going to lose Micah. And the even larger fear, the one that makes it hard to sleep most nights, is that if that happens, we're going to lose everything.

I check behind the couch, behind the curtains, under his bed. Micah tends to fall asleep in weird places. It took him a long time to get used to sleeping in a bed. The adoption agency didn't tell my parents much, only that he had a hard time of it after his mother died, drifting from relative to relative until he just drifted out of his family altogether and into a state-run orphanage. His life in the *dyet dom* in Russia is why he can't sleep at night. That's why when he does, it's usually when he's hidden away somewhere. I keep checking. Hall closet, my room, Shana's, my father's. I don't call out for him, because if he's asleep, it'll scare him. That's the other thing about Micah. If it's bad when he's sleeping, it's sometimes worse when he wakes up.

The phone rings. It's Shana, breathless, scared. And somehow hearing her voice like that, all small and far away, makes me even more frightened. "Did you find him?" she asks, and I can hear the rush of cars in the street, the clang of the harbor bells, tinny through her cell.

"He's not here," I say, then I take a breath. "We should call Dad."

"No," she says. Her voice is flat, featureless. This is not up for discussion. "Not yet. Not there. We'll find him."

"Do you want me to meet you?" I ask, suddenly wanting to get out of here, wanting to be with her.

"Wait there. In case he comes back. I'll check down by the water." And she's gone. I keep looking. The pantry, hoping he's curled around a box of cereal, asleep. The thing is, I passed the door to Mom's studio half a dozen times as I crisscrossed the apartment. I wish I could say that it hadn't occurred to me that he'd be in there hidden away with the

Chloe

stacks of stretched canvases and the jars of paintbrushes, but it had. I just didn't want to look. I haven't been in there since Dad took her to the hospital for an evaluation, which turned into a short stay, which turned into permanent care. It wasn't what some people might think. She wasn't dragged away screaming and fighting, arms bound in a straitjacket. Dad simply told her they were going to the beach. Then instead of heading up the coast to Popham Beach or Wolf's Neck, they drove inland, away from the water, toward Augusta.

I stand in front of the door for a minute, willing myself to put my hand on the doorknob and turn it, but I can't. Shana wasn't home when they left for the hospital. She was already out, away, disconnected from the rest of us. I was there, watching as Mom packed her beach bag, putting in her beach sneakers and her floppy hat and her worn beach towel, the image of a lobster just barely still outlined against the pink sand. She was happy, excited to be going, like a kid. Dad didn't tell me where they were going, but I knew something was wrong, could see it in his eyes, when he told me to watch Micah, pressing a twenty into my hand for the toy store.

I imagine they drove for a bit, up the highway, still heading north, my mother drifting in and out, her dreams folding into her thoughts, constantly asking where they were going as her brain slipped from memory into imaginings and back again. I imagine that she asked my father if he was sure they were headed in the right direction. If maybe he wasn't the one who was confused, lowering her visor against the afternoon sun as they slipped past the exits to the water and made their way through the trees. I wonder if she kept her tote bag, still slightly sandy from the beach, between her feet as my father talked with the doctors, explaining her condition. Did she keep interrupting him to ask about the ocean, about the fishing boats moored offshore, about the angel sitting in the corner, watching them? Did he tell her he'd wait there for her while she talked to the doctors? Keep her bag for her so she wouldn't misplace it? Did he kiss her good-bye, waving, smiling as she walked down the hall away from him?

I touch the doorknob, which feels cool against my hand. I know I have to check, see if he's in there asleep on the love seat or curled up in the corner, his head resting on the beach bag, breathing in the smell of salt and sand and her. The glass knob is loose under my fingers. I have to turn it all the way to the right then pull. The door has always stuck slightly. I close my eyes and press inward, feeling the door shift. A loud *thunk* behind me makes me stop. The sound of boots dropping on the wood floor. One then two then three then four.

"Chloe?" Shana's voice fills the apartment. I pull the door shut. "Chloe?" Louder this time. I turn and walk toward her voice, to the living room, where she's standing holding Micah's hand. He looks up at me slowly, watching

Chloe

my face. "He was down at the pier," she says. "I asked him what he was doing, but he wouldn't answer me. Wouldn't answer Vernon either." He squirms away from Shana's hand and crosses to where I am standing.

"Are you okay?" I ask, reaching out to touch his cheek. I realize I'm asking if he's okay in the sense that our family now understands okay, not the way most people think about it. Shana watches us, arms folded, her mouth a thin line on her face.

"You can't just run off like that," Shana says. Her voice is too loud, bouncing off the ceiling and the walls, ricocheting back at us. Micah reaches for my hand, wraps his fingers tightly around mine, almost painfully. "You can't just take off without telling anyone where you're going. When you'll be back." Micah squeezes my fingers even harder, making me wince a little. "Didn't you think we'd worry when you just snuck out? What if something happened to you?" This hangs in the air between us, so solid we can almost touch it. Shana looks up at me, daring me to say something, but I don't. She's right. Something could have happened. "Say something," she says, looking back at Micah. He turns away from her and presses his face against my arm.

"Shana, stop," I say. "He gets it."

"What a surprise. You're taking his side against me."

"There aren't sides. I agree with you, but is this really the best way to do this? You're scaring him." She refuses to look back at Micah.

"Why is it that I scare him? Why does he always come to you?"

"Shana, you can't expect him to come to you when you're gone all the time." I squeeze Micah's hand and look down at him.

"What are you saying?" she asks, squinting at me.

"I'm just saying that telling him he can't take off all the time seems a little ironic coming from you."

"Four is a lot different than fifteen," she says.

"And mid-afternoon is a lot different than the middle of the night," I say. I feel the tug of Micah's hand and look down at him.

"God, Chloe, you aren't my—" She stops and looks down at her feet. I feel the undertow of panic threaten to pull me under, but I hold on tightly to my anger, letting myself float on it.

"What were you going to say, Shana?" I ask, but she won't look at me. "Were you going to tell me that I'm not your mother?" Shana works her fingers against the frayed cuff of her sweater, trying to pull it down to cover her hand. I can see the shift in her, too, as she looks up at me, trying to cling to that same raft. The raft of our argument, keeping us from sinking into our sadness. She turns and heads toward the entry hall. "You're going out?" I ask, watching as she pulls on her boots. She doesn't answer me as she pushes her arms into her coat sleeves and twists her scarf around her neck. "What a surprise," I say, willing her to stay. Yell at me, argue with me, anything just as long as she doesn't go away. She pulls the door shut behind her, a soft *whoosh* and then a click. Not even a slam to punctuate her leaving.

"Are you hungry?" I ask, looking down at Micah. He nods at me. Always hungry. Always up for a snack. "Let's get out of here," I say. Because suddenly I can understand the feeling that Shana must have. Like if we stay in this apartment for one more second, I'll start crying or screaming or both. If we just sit and wait for my father to come home, listen as he shuffles his stocking feet across the wood floor, watch as he slowly gathers his flannel Bean coat and his wool hat and his cigarettes before heading out onto the roof, we will slowly start to sink. And sometimes I think if we let ourselves go under too far, if we stop treading for too long, we'll just keep sinking farther down into the inky darkness until we don't have the energy to kick back up to the surface.

It's way too cold to be out. The wind whips in between the buildings, blowing at us from every direction, up the sleeves of our coats, down the backs of our necks. We bend our heads down, trying to press our chins into the swirls of our scarves and the necks of our jackets, feeling the bite of frost on the tips of our noses and the tops of our cheeks. Sometimes when it's this cold you can even feel it in your teeth, like when you've been chewing ice for too long or when you take too big of a bite from your ice-cream cone.

"Just to the end of the block," I tell Micah, my voice muffled by my scarf. I can't tell if he has heard me or not. His eyes are watering from the wind. The snow, packed by footsteps and snow shovels, feels hard through the soles of my boots. I grab Micah's arm as he slips a bit on an icy patch created by a steaming vent on the edge of the sidewalk. "Here," I say, pointing to a brightly lit door on the edge of a building. I tug the steel handle, letting Micah step into the warmth first. We pull off our hats and mittens and stuff them into the pockets of our coats. We're surrounded by the smells of cinnamon and chocolate and coffee. I unzip my coat, letting the heat push against my sweater and into my skin. "Order whatever you want," I tell Micah. He opens his eyes at me, making me think for the seventeenth time in two days that he understands way more than he lets on. "Well," I say, smiling at him, "don't go too nuts. I only have ten dollars."

The loud screech of a guitar followed by a scream makes me jump.

"Turn it *down*!" a guy behind the counter yells. The volume lowers a bit, but the music doesn't change. Power cords and drums vibrate through the speakers. Micah and I walk up to the counter. "Is it still too loud?" the guy asks. "I can ask her to turn it down."

"It's okay," I say. Micah walks over to the display case and bends down to see everything stacked inside.

"I lost a bet, so we have to listen to this," he says in apology.

"You did not just lose a bet," Raven says, pushing through the back door. "You lost THE bet." She smiles at me, and for a moment I think she isn't going to recognize me. "Hey, Chloe, right?" she says, leaning against the counter. She tilts her head for a moment, angling her ear toward the speaker mounted into the ceiling above us. The guy turns and begins filling a carafe with milk. "Don't you just love Guns n' Roses?" she asks.

"No," he says, screwing the top on the carafe and starting to fill another one with cream.

"Don't mind Todd," she says, smiling at me. "He's just grouchy because I totally nailed the lunchtime trivia."

"Only because it was a song from the '80s," Todd says, bending down to put the milk jug and the cream carton into the refrigerator. "Let me ask you," he says, turning to address me, "what song was number one in 1981?"

"That's not fair," Raven says. "She wasn't even alive in 1981."

"Neither were you," he says, pointing a coffee stirrer in her direction. Micah slides farther down the case, checking out the cookies now. "Okay then. Do you know?" he asks, looking back at me.

One thing about my parents, they are 1980s freaks. Well,

were. We have DVDs of every John Hughes movie, plus all these CDs of bands like The Cure and Depeche Mode. Shana's middle name is Lisa because of that chick in *Weird Science* (Dad picked it), and mine is Samantha for Molly Ringwald's character in *Sixteen Candles* (Mom picked it). My parents used to snuggle on the couch and watch those movies over and over or listen to their CDs in the dark, late at night.

"'Bette Davis Eyes,' by Kim Carnes," I say.

Todd just looks at me for about ten seconds before he says anything.

"I give up," he says, shaking his head and making his way around the front of the counter with a box of sugar and sweetener packets.

"Man," Raven says, smiling at me. "That was sweet, Chloe." She flips her towel over her shoulder and leans forward to look at Micah making his way back toward us. "So . . ." She looks at me.

"Micah," I say.

"So, Micah, what'll it be?" she asks him. He just smiles and points to the pile of cinnamon scones. "Good choice," she says. "Those are my favorite." She slips the biggest scone off the pile and places it on a plate. "And coffee?" she asks.

"Two," I say. "One mostly milk."

"And the other with cream. Right?" she asks. I nod and slip the ten out of my pocket. Raven turns and places the mugs on the counter in front of me. "Oh no," she says, waving my money away. "This is on Todd." Then louder. "Todd, I'm taking my break now."

She unties the strings of her apron and hangs it on a hook by the door to the back room. I hand the plate with the scone on it to Micah and pick up the two cups. The door behind me opens as the only two other customers leave. "Pounce," Raven says over her shoulder at me. I raise my eyebrows, not sure what she means. "The purple chairs. They're open." Micah hurries over to the overstuffed purple chairs and plops down in the one closest to the window. I follow him and settle into the other one, putting our cups on the table between us. Raven pulls up a third chair, this one green, and lowers herself into it. "So Chloe," Raven says, blowing across the top of her coffee. "What's your story?" I freeze for a moment, suspended between wanting to tell her everything and just getting up and running out the door. Raven tilts her head at me, watching. "Start with just one thing," she says.

CHAPTER EIGHT

Shana

AFTER MOM WENT off to the hospital, it was probably a month before Dad told us she wasn't coming back. I think about that when I'm walking around Old Port, and I see those notices for a lost dog. Sometimes people tape a photo of the dog to the notice, and they offer a reward and they make it so you can tear off the phone number and take it with you. I always think about how hard they worked, making copies of the picture so they could have lots of signs to put around everywhere, and doing all that cutting and writing and taping. Once I saw one on cardboard all wrapped in cellophane, to keep the rain off. How hopeful they must have been at first, so careful with their tape and their cellophane. If you're *that* careful, God has to bring your dog back, isn't that the deal? Or maybe not, maybe some voice inside them is saying the signs need to last a long damn time—when something is lost, it tends to stay that way.

But the signs I always notice are the ones that have turned to crap, all wrinkled up, bleached from the sun, the ink in dried streaks, and there's the dog, and he's bleached out, too, still looking at you, still lost. That was pretty much me and Chlo, after Mom left—dusting the house every day, stealing fresh flowers for the kitchen table (a funeral home has no end of fresh flowers), hopeful as hell. Those beaten-up signs—I always wonder if the people just finally gave up, or maybe, *maybe*, the dog got found and they just blew off taking the signs down. I like to think that. I remember how it felt the first time we didn't bother to vacuum or dust, how we noticed but just didn't say anything, like we'd slowly gotten as tattered and bleached out as one of those missing-dog notices. And all of us still lost without her.

The first time I had to meet with the social worker, that was one of her questions: *What has been your worst day since everything happened?* And I said the day we didn't steal flowers, that was the worst. The day the vase just sat, upside down in the dish drainer. I don't think it's the answer she wanted, so I am trying to study up, like for a test at school, because they are coming back soon, only about a week from now, and this is the biggest test ever, pretty much.

I wish they would ask me the best day, before everything happened. That one is easy.

Dad still had his pickup truck from when he did pottery, the one with one big dent in each door, and the Yosemite Sam mud flaps and the old bumper sticker that said, I'M NOT

AFRAID OF HELL . . . I'M FROM TEXAS, and the tailgate that you had to slam three times before it would close. One night he packed a big cooler into the bed and let me and Chlo ride in the bed, too, tied in with rope for seat belts, and he drove us out, bumping over the country roads around all these curves, while he and Mom sat right up close to each other in the front seat, and every time one of us knocked on the little window, Mom would turn around and act like she was shocked to see us there, so that we did it like twenty-five times in a row. And then it was dusk and we pulled into the Bel-Air Drive-In Theatre, where they had this dusk-to-dawn showing, six movies in a row, and I asked if we were going to see all six, and Dad said, you bet we are, no punking out for us, and pulled backward into a spot on the gravel on the back row so that the tires crunched under us, and then he had to tune the radio to this one special station on AM, which broadcast the soundtrack for the movies. And he slid open the little window long enough to point out the brick projection tower, and he said how those were the dumbest radio waves on earth because all they had to do was travel like a hundred yards, but they still went ahead and went all the way into outer space, for nothing. And that was when Chlo was just eight and she was so into space stuff it wasn't funny, had memorized the planets and everything, and she couldn't stop talking about the radio waves, even after the movies started. The whole place smelled like popcorn and pizza and corn dogs, and we bought all of those plus king-size Three Musketeers at the snack bar, all lit up with yellow lights and hung all over with loudspeakers that kept saying there would be no refunds and that alcoholic beverages were prohibited and that everyone should turn off their lights, including their parking lights. I remember it felt like the beginning of something, settling in under a blanket with a Coke and a corn dog, and the guy made the announcements again, and for the first time in my life I felt like the world held possibility, that things could happen. Except then, right then, I was only thinking of good things. Stupid.

We saw all six movies, just like Dad said we would, even though most of the other cars were gone by movie three, *Attack of the Giant Leeches*, and by movie four, *Tarzan and the She-Devil*, we were one of just three cars in the whole lot. My dad loved those old movies the way my mom loved all the stuff from the 1980s, and they were a deadly team at Trivial Pursuit . . . I mean, no one could beat them. By when the last movie ended, I woke up just in time for the closing credits, the sky just beginning to go to light gray over the horizon, teenage boys moving across the lot, picking up trash with a nail on a stick, the birds starting to chirp as the film ran dark. Chloe slept beside me under a blanket, her fingers still curled around a paper plate, and Mom and Dad had left their lawn chairs sometime in the night and were also asleep, in the front seat of the truck, Mom's head in the curve of his neck, and his hand on her leg. I stood, sore from the truck bed, and stretched, and just looked around me, seeing a little corner of orange at the bottom of the sky, and I stretched, stretched my arms out as far as I could, as if it would always be the start of a day, and I wanted to keep it the way Chloe keeps her glass in jars—the low mist of fog rolling over the gravel, the grass and popcorn boxes flattened by tire tracks, the movie screen rippling a little in the breeze, dew on the roof of the truck, and my family all around me, safe and asleep.

When Chlo was little and we got into a fight, she used to crawl into my bed late at night and sleep next to me. She wouldn't even get under the blanket, because she didn't want to disturb me, and she's always been so small that I would wake up in the morning and feel her balled up next to me and think that I'd left my winter coat or a blanket on the bed, until she would whisper, "I'm sorry," still half-asleep. It has probably been five years since she did that, and the funny part is that now Micah will go sleep in her room when he's upset. But he never gets in the bed because, the social worker told us, he's not used to beds. He's used to the floor, and that's where he usually sleeps. I guess it's whatever you get used to.

It has been two days since we yelled at each other, and I can't stand it. I can't stand passing in the hall without talking, and I can't stand that she won't play Slow Walking, and I can't stand when she comes to the top of the stairs and tells Vernon to tell me that one of my friends called, even though I'm standing right there. I mean, I know it's stupid, but it keeps hollowing me out, every occasion of silence, emptying me out by spoonfuls.

And so I decide this is the day—I'm taking her out with me tonight, whether she likes it or not. And we are going all out, and she is going to be the freakiest chick in all of Portland, and I swear she's going to love it. She'll get inside it, see how hidden she is, and love it. I swear.

A half hour later I'm in my room listening to Massive Attack cranked up to like nine, and tearing through all my drawers and closets, because nothing is going to fit her. Okay, the spiked collars will fit, and probably I have a pair of fishnets for her, but the rest—nothing, zip. And there is one store in all of downtown that sells the right stuff, and it's wicked expensive and closed, so I'm screwed anyway. So that means bus number forty-nine to the mall, and in a half hour I'm there. The first score is a pair of pretty cool chunky boots at Shoe Show, then a decent handcuff bracelet at the Piercing Pagoda, then, without even trying, like, with one hand tied behind my back, I come on this totally wack-ass pleated black velvet miniskirt in *Sears* of all places. It's going to look great, but if Chlo ever says where I got it, I am going to look like the biggest dork in the world.

Actually, I probably look like that now. I mean, I never go to the mall unless it's with Jason and Blaine and Magenta, sometimes Sammy, totally Goth'd out—lace, chains, capes, huge hair, six-inch boots—just to goof on people. "Some people collect stamps," Blaine always pronounces. "We collect the pitiless stares of the masses." He'll say crap like that, then he wants to buy a cinnamon-sugar pretzel and has to borrow money to do so. So today is probably the first time in a year I have been here just as *me*, and kind of yuck-me, too—Cheap Trick T-shirt, one of Dad's old cardigans, jeans, Vans, hair in a ponytail. It's startling when I catch myself in a mirror, like I expect to see me and don't, and instead it's some version of me, like the me I dreamed once and then forgot about. I'm some kind of sideways vampire, unable to see my reflection. I walk around, and carry bags, and I buy my own pretzel (jalapeño, with melty cheese), and old ladies smile at me, and sometimes boys check me out, then pretend like they're just reading my T-shirt. God, so dumb. I stand for a while and watch the little kids moving up and down on the trucks and ponies and dragons, the kind you put a quarter in to ride for three minutes, and I wonder if Micah would like it, if it would scare him the way so much else seems to. And then I don't want to be thinking about him, I don't want to be thinking about Dad, who came to breakfast with his usual postvisit hangover, and who I heard in an argument with Vernon about an hour before I left the house. A real argument, both of them shouting. It sounded bad.

I shake all of that out of my head, then throw all my change in the fountain, which I figure entitles me to about seventy-eight wishes, and I buy an Orange Julius, and I watch some little kids spin a wheel to see if they win free fries or a free vanilla cone. The free cone seems to be the money prize. I check out the new cars parked at the far end and wonder again how they get them into the mall, and I know all the time how Jason says that if all the malls collapsed at once, the collective intelligence of the country would rise exponentially, but I don't care. I like it here. I mean, I like it and I don't. I know the mall is just a lot of fake plants and fake food and people buying crap for too much money, and at Christmas people pay for their kids to talk to Santa, learning greed the way some kids learn piano. I know all that. I can hear the Muzak, smell the waffle fries. Like everybody else, I walk around stuck inside a cliché, like we're the stars of some TV show we plan to watch later, if nothing else is on. But still, there's something hopeful about this place, too, and maybe it takes having a crazy mother to get that. People buy stuff, because they think they are going to need it, because they think their lives are going to keep skipping down the same old path, and I want so much for that to be true for them that it nearly makes me cry. The mall says, *Nothing is terrible.* The mall says, *Life is small and adequate.* Blaine and Jason and Magenta hate all that, because they want things to be dark, things to be black, because black is huge and bottomless, and they are drawn to it like little kids peering down a well. Because they don't know. They never fell in.

On the way out I pass by the store that sells NASCAR miniatures, right next to Chick-fil-A, which I always love because they have these signs making a big self-righteous deal of how they are closed on Sundays, while ignoring the fact that their store name sounds like a variety of cat food. I smile, as always, walking past, and then I notice one of the boys behind the counter there, wearing his pointed paper hat, his Chick-fil-A smock, and he's staring at me. And not staring at me like the other boys, not checking me out, but staring like maybe he's trying to place me, and I'm thinking maybe I know him from school, but no. He's cute enough, I'd remember. I mean, his face is just kinda normal, but he's standing there under that pointy hat, holding a paper bag he just shook open, looking like he wants to wave at me but afraid he'd get in trouble with the assistant manager if he did. Cute.

A few hours later, we've managed to dye the tips of Chloe's hair, and it looks awesome. Manic Panic Atomic Turquoise, and when she swings her head around, the tips swirl out in this ring of color, like a carousel. And only the tips, because she says that tomorrow morning, first thing, she is cutting it off. Whatever, I tell her. She looks great. I start in on her face with the lily white cream powder and then heavy kohl around her eyes, black rose lipstick. She keeps cutting her eyes toward the mirror behind her.

"Don't look yet," I tell her.

"This is stupid. All this, and I don't even get trick-or-treat candy."

"Shut up. I'll buy you some candy."

I give her my best collar and get her into one of my sliced-up Smiths T-shirts and some lace sleeves and the whack-ass skirt from Sears and the bracelet and the fishnets and the chunky boots, and then I tell her to stand in front of my mirror.

"Wow," she says. She keeps looking at herself, almost touching her face, then stopping. I remember how it felt for me the first time, being transformed, being someone else.

"Cool, huh?"

"I totally look like I could kick someone's ass," she says.

"Okay, Chlo? Goths are pretty much nonviolent, so if you go around talking like that, the others aren't going to like it."

"Ooh, how awful that would be," she says.

"Chlo . . ."

"I'll be good, I promise." She looks at herself again, turns to both sides. "Shana, why do you do this?"

I want to tell her, to say how it's like those movies where a prisoner makes a mannequin of himself and leaves it in his bed while he tunnels out through the wall and makes his escape, how the makeup and clothes are just like that, something propped up to fool everyone while I dig deeper and deeper inside myself, trying to escape. But how can I tell her that? She's like some little kid who gets told that her dead pet has just run away to a happy life on a farm some-where. I smile at her in the mirror.

"Because it's cool. Wait until you hear some of the music. Plus, I know what you think, but give them a chance tonight. They really are pretty cool."

She nods. "I'll try. But one thing, can we not go to Star-bucks?" I start to ask, and she quickly says, "I mean, Star-bucks is kinda lame and corporate, right?"

"Yeah, okay," I tell her. "No Starbucks."

Sometime near midnight, Blaine decides he's hungry and Sammy wants coffee, and I have to talk them out of Star-bucks. I think of this other place I can't remember the name of that's on the south end of Old Port near the used bookstore, a place with green stools at the counter and pool tables in the back, and they sell hot dogs and snack foods. It has a hand-lettered sign in the window saying they have the hottest coffee in town. I don't know if hotness is what I look for in coffee first, and even walking by the door the place smells a little bit bad, but why not? Like Chlo said, Starbucks is probably the kind of place we're supposed to hate. Blaine wants to know if this other place has biscotti, and I tell him I'd be willing to bet they don't.

So far it has been a really good night, the best one I can remember in a long time. At first, the others had no clue it was Chloe I had with me, and for a while she went along, saying she was this new kid in the high school, that she'd just moved here from New Zealand and had no accent because she'd been part of a university experiment and was raised in a lab for her first eight years. Finally it was Jason who said, "Man, you suck, *Chloe*," and she laughed, and all of us forgot what we were supposed to be and laughed too, all our dark mouths splitting open. Jason has his hair looking just like Robert Smith from The Cure, and they all tell Chloe she looks awesome, and I make a big show of saying *thank you* every time they compliment her. We walk all around Old Port, down Pearl Street and Commercial Street, past the waterfront, where we sit on our usual wall and watch the lights on the tanker ships way out in the ocean, guessing where they were going, what they carry. And when it gets cold we head off near the park and then down Duran Street, and Chloe asks if she could just carry one of Magenta's clove cigs, and I make her promise to never, ever smoke, and so she does, and Jason says they should have named it Duran Duran Street, and we all tell him he's lame, and Blaine says he is hungry like the wolf for a chocolate biscotti. We laugh, and we keep laughing, forget to complain about the world for one night, and the air is chilly and full of the smells of the ocean, and somehow it's like Chloe's presence has made things better, made us all hopeful in some way, and I think she feels that, too.

Even now as we make our way toward Charlie's Rec Room (after I finally remember the name of the place), Chloe keeps letting her shoulder bump my arm, and once she even hooks her little finger through mine and gives it a squeeze, and when we turn the corner on State Street, Chloe announces a Slow Walking contest. I jump right in, taking the smallest of baby steps, Chloe taking smaller ones yet, laughing while the others walk ahead and Jason walks backward, watching us, telling us that our game is just a metaphor for a fear of death, and Chloe tells him to shut up and everyone laughs again, and Chloe looks up at me through her heavy dark eyes, and whispers that she's winning, and I say no I am, and then, from up ahead, in the shadows down State Street, I hear a voice say *you fucking freaks*, and then I hear Blaine say *just keep walking*. We give up our contest and run ahead as fast as we can, our feet splashing in the dirty water along the gutter, until we are with the others standing in the red glow of neon light from the beer signs in the bar window, and they are spilling out of the door and surrounding us, their Budweiser caps pulled low or worn backward, their flannel shirts whipping in the breeze, and one of them calls us freaks again, like he's searching for a better word but is too stupid or drunk to think of one, and another one says we are witches and another calls us Marilyn Manson, like that makes any sense, and I can feel my heart pounding inside my chest. I take Chloe's hand and wish we were home. I wish it hard, with my eyes closed half a second, like a real wish from a fairy tale, and when I open my eyes Blaine and Jason are trying to push past, Jason telling us over his shoulder to just ignore them and keep go-

ing, only we can't, and then Sammy says something I can't hear, and one of them throws his beer bottle down against the curb and grabs Sammy and shoves him back across the same curb, holding him up and pushing him along at the same time and under the dull thud of my own beating heart I hear Magenta screaming for them to stop it, to leave us alone and Chloe is gripping my hand and pulling me back and then there is a hand in my hair yanking it sideways and I scream and Chloe's hand falls away from me, and I keep noticing the smell of the spilled beer, notice that my stockings tear as my knee hits the pavement, notice that some of them are wearing work boots all muddy with the buckles loose, watching all of it in slow motion and then I look up and see one of the hands grab the collar around Chloe's neck and yank it free, and she just says, *ow*, like it's a bee sting, and then other hands are pushing her, pushing all of us, and I hear the first punch land in the dense folds of Jason's trench coat, the air forced out of him, and Blaine is crying, and somewhere behind us other people are shouting *break it up, break it up*, and as I am yanked backward into all those hands, the last thing I see is Chloe, covering her head with her arms, sinking down into all that black.

CHAPTER NINE

Chloe

WE GOT OFF better than the rest of them. Two of the three men who jumped us were lying on the sidewalk, held there by men from inside the bar. The third took off down the street. "God damn kids," one of the guys from the bar said, his voice hoarse and low. Old episodes of Scooby-Doo ran through my head. "If it weren't for you meddling kids . . ."

"I called the police," a woman said from the doorway. "They're sending an ambulance, too." I watched everything like I was supposed to be figuring out the meaning of what I was seeing. I kept thinking that at some point someone was going to walk out of the bar and shout *Cut* and we'd have to do it all again and keep doing it until we got it right.

"Shana, we have to go," I said close to her ear. She was sitting on the curb, right where I went down, sliding her finger along the streak of white makeup that my cheek had left on the sidewalk. "Shana," I said again when she didn't look up. "We can't afford to be here." She looked up at me and nodded. People from the bar stood around talking, the guys who jumped us sitting against the wall. I kept looking at their faces, trying to read their lips as they murmured. Shana stood slowly, looking across to where Jason was standing, holding the front of his shirt up to his nose, the blood not even visible on all the black. He nodded at her before turning to accept a Baggie filled with ice from one of the waitresses. I stepped off the curb, watching as a piece of glass spun out from under my boot, sliding across the ice and into the road where it glinted in the light spilling from the bar. We kept walking up the street, our shadows lengthening and then shrinking in the streetlights. Giant us. Tiny us. Taller then shorter then taller again. I didn't turn around or say anything, only felt the pressure of Shana's hand on the small of my back.

Shana's knee is a mess. So is her left palm. Furrowed and broken like a freshly plowed field. Although this field is red and angry without promise. I shiver in the cold bathroom, goose bumps covering my arms and legs. I can still feel Shana's fingers on my face and my neck where she helped me wash off the makeup. The washcloth was warm and rough as it slid across my skin. She worked slowly, silently, looking at my cheek, my neck. Never my eyes. Her fingers gently probed my face, feeling if anything was broken. Now I sit on the edge of the tub, a towel wrapped around me as she splashes water on her face and her neck, finding her own skin beneath the white. "You should go to bed," she says. The first time she has spoken. I nod and stand, pulling my towel tighter around me. She leans forward against the sink as I pass. Inches away from me, but too far to touch.

I'm naked except for my tank top and underwear, staring at myself in the full-length mirror nailed to the back of my bedroom door. My clothes a bumpy black mound in the corner. I touch the pink ring around my neck. It hurts. A lot. I'm lucky the collar had a weak buckle. I turn my face one way and then the other. The left side is swollen where my cheek hit the edge of the curb. The man in the denim jacket who helped me up said I was lucky, it could have been a lot worse. And it's that phrase that keeps poking at me in the dark as I try to fall asleep. *It could have been a lot worse.*

"So, what's on the agenda for today?" my father asks, taking a box of Rice Krispies from the pantry. He slides his finger under the top then reaches inside to unfold the bag before plunking it down in front of Micah.

"Nothing much," I say, leaning over my cereal. In this position my hair spills forward across my cheeks, hiding the crescent-shaped bruise that is slowly turning maroon and dark purple. The blue tips of my hair startle me as my hair slides past my eyes. I take a bite of my toast and look across at Micah, who is slowly spooning sugar over his cereal, so much that it is starting to form a white mound in the middle. My father is leaning against the counter, his eyes closed. His coffee raised halfway to his mouth.

I reach across and put my hand on Micah's wrist. "That's enough," I whisper softly. He looks up at me and smiles and I smile back, forgetting my cheek for a moment. But the pressure on my bruised skin makes me wince.

"Chlo-ee," Micah says, reaching up to touch his own face. I shake my head, letting my hair fall back across my cheek, then smile at him again. This time smaller.

"Eat up, little man," my father says, turning to switch the coffeemaker off. "We have a lot to do before this afternoon." Micah takes a bite of cereal, letting most of it spill off his spoon and dribble back into the bowl. On the next one he hits the corner of his mouth, tipping the whole spoonful. A tear drops down his cheek, mixing in with the cereal floating in the sugary sea.

"It's okay," I say, reaching out to touch Micah's wrist again. He blinks fast, sending more tears spilling from his eyes and into the bowl. My father lifts the faucet handle, letting water splash into his coffee cup before setting it in the sink.

"All right," he says, ruffling Micah's hair as he passes. "Five minutes and we need to leave. First a haircut. Then the mall. We need to find pants that actually fit you." Shana is leaning against the doorjamb, watching, her arms folded. "Hey, sleepyhead," he says, walking past her toward his bedroom. Shana fills a mug with the remains of the coffee, careful not to use her left hand, and sits down at the table. Micah looks up at her, his eyes still wet. She looks at him for a moment, frowning, and then up at me. She takes a sip of her coffee, studying my cheek and trying to look past the collar of my turtleneck. Micah attempts a couple more bites of cereal, but his hand is shaking too badly and most of it ends up back in the bowl. He gets up and puts the bowl in the sink.

"Micah," I say, making him pause at the door. "It really is okay." He doesn't look at me, but instead walks to the front hall and begins pulling on his coat. I think to remind him to brush his teeth, but decide not to. Shana keeps sipping her coffee, letting it sit in her mouth for a moment before she swallows. We both sit quietly as our father puts on his boots and coat and helps Micah with his mittens.

"Don't forget," he calls. We hear the front door open, sending a draft swirling through the apartment. "Tomorrow." Shana sniffs slightly and I look at her quickly, thinking she's crying, but she's sipping her coffee again. Tiny sips. Her lips a thin line across the rim of the cup. The door shuts with a thunk, and the apartment is quiet again. Silent except for the popping of the coffeemaker slowly cooling down and the sound of Shana slowly drinking, one tiny sip at a time. I push away from the table and head toward my room. I need to get out of here again. I slide one of my mother's old wool sweaters from the shelf in my closet

Chloe

and pull it over my head, feeling the pressure on my neck as I push my arms through the sleeves. This one is navy blue and fraying along the cuffs. Splattered here and there with white paint so it almost looks like it is supposed to be that way. A starry sky on a moonless night. Shana steps into my room and sits on the end of my bed, pulling my quilt over her legs.

"Like we don't both have this huge calendar in our heads with the day circled in red with arrows all around it." She spreads her palms against my quilt, trying to make each hand fit into one of the blocks.

"He's trying," I say, rolling up the cuffs of the sweater, folding the frayed ends under so they're not visible.

"A trip to the barber then a run through Sears for a new pair of pants." She turns her left hand over and studies her palm, the lines still visible, but darker now. "Twenty bucks says he gets Micah a Happy Meal at the food court."

"What's wrong with that?" I ask, pulling my hair up behind my head before twisting an elastic around the bundle. I tuck the aqua-colored ends under, so they're hidden.

"It's like he's trying to make everything look so normal, but it's just an illusion. I mean we were both *right* there in front of him, both with scratches and bruises and marks and he didn't even notice. It's like if we can just pull it together for the visitation, we can be as screwed up as we want to be the rest of the time." I run my fingers over my cheekbone, feeling the swollen skin, but stop when I see Shana looking at me. "Like if we sit still, he can capture this one moment in time and then frame it and hang it over the mantel."

"He's trying to keep Micah safe," I say, turning to look at her. "Trying to make sure they don't take him away."

"So that's it then? That's our standard? As long as Micah stays here, we're okay?"

"It's a start."

"It sucks," she says, pushing the quilt off her legs and standing up.

"At least he's doing something."

"Sometimes something is just as bad as nothing. Maybe worse." She walks past me and toward the door.

"Shana?" I whisper, not turning around.

"Yeah?" she says just as softly.

"We are going to be okay. Aren't we?" I fold my fingers over the cuffs of my sweater. The only answer she gives me is the sound of footsteps. A low noise that keeps getting softer until it disappears.

Maybe if she had been a normal mother, soccer mom, PTA, aerobics at noon Monday, Wednesday, and Friday, we could have seen it sooner, but we had no way of knowing that the blue dinners she always served on the night of the full moon were because an angel told her to. She'd smile as she'd ladle blue potato soup into bowls nestled in a flower of blue corn chips. Shana would always argue that the fruit salad of blue plums and blueberries and grapes was actually cheating because the grapes weren't actually blue, but a dark shade of purple. Mom would even tint the crust on the blueberry pie blue so that it looked strange and exotic settling in beside a scoop of ice cream. Blueberry, of course.

The counselors told us that we were lucky she heard benevolent voices—angels, God, the Virgin Mary—and not the darker voices that some schizophrenics hear. Hers told her to paint, walk along the ocean, and make strange meals for us. Sometimes she woke us in the middle of the night to sample muffins she had made from the rhubarb she picked in the garden or tea brewed from the rose hips that grew wild along the beach. The voices and the creatures that visited her were ruthless though. They never let her sleep. They barely let her eat. And one time they almost killed her. That was when our father decided to move us to Portland.

It worked for a while. We had new schools, a new routine. I even heard them talking about taking a trip together. Just the two of them. *Somewhere warm*, she said to him, pressing her face into his neck. Shana and I would lie in my bed sometimes, feeling the cold from the open window on our faces and listening to our parents laughing in the living room. My mother's laugh, loud and unbridled, spilling across the wood floors and under the doorways. My father's laugh, deep and careful, blanketing us. We heard them whispering late into the night, too soft to hear the words, just the rhythms. The notes spilling across us and coaxing us to sleep. We had Halloween. Jack-o'-lanterns flickering from the windows. Witches sailing across the moon. Then Thanksgiving. Our annual hike around Bubble Pond in Bar Harbor, thermoses filled with hot chocolate tucked into our daypacks. Then Christmas. *No electricity on Christmas Eve*, she always said, flipping switches and lighting candles. Board games and popcorn until midnight. Then bed. *I think I hear Santa* she would always say, even when we were past believing.

In the spring we had Micah to look forward to. The letters from the social workers, the adoption agencies, the counselors. *We'll take any child*, my mother told them. *Boy, girl, age doesn't matter*. Everyone wants babies. Cute and lovable and without issues. Our family knows that's not how life works. Sometimes your first chance isn't your only chance. At least that's the way it seemed then.

If only we had gone to Starbucks. The worst that happens in there is maybe the jitters or a sugar high. The honey-colored countertops. The stainless steel racks featuring lip balm and seasonal merchandise and biscotti to go. The purple and yellow and green pendant lights. The overstuffed chairs. The tiny tables. All seemingly random and funky and a little bohemian, but really researched by design and marketing and sales so that even while you are drinking a cup of coffee, you are thinking about your next cup. The feeling that even when you are enjoying your life, it would be so much better if you could just have a little bit more.

I tell myself it's only because I'm desperate. I need to do something about my face. I can't trust that my hair will cover it while we're meeting with the social worker. I can't ask Shana. She's so pissed off at Dad, at everything right now, that she might just tell me to leave it. *Let her see us for what we really are.* I watch Raven and Todd through the window. He scowls at her and she swishes her towel at him. Sometimes I watch TV like that—on mute, so only facial expressions and actions can tell the story. I press against the same door that Micah and I entered. Only a few days ago, but when something like last night happens, it's as if everything exists on one side of it or the other. My mother's hospitalization is like that, too. Like I was one person before and now I'm another barely resembling the thing I used to be.

"Chloe," Raven says.

"Don't say anything," Todd says, pointing in my direction before turning back to Raven. "Okay. Answer the question."

"I still have eight minutes."

"You either know it or you don't."

"The rules state that we each have ten minutes to answer the questions."

"Let me know when you're ready," Todd says, sliding past her and toward the door to the back. He scoops a handful of cookie chunks from the sample plate near the register and drops several in his mouth. "Seven minutes," he says around a mouthful of triple chocolate chunk.

"Honestly," Raven says, slapping her towel against the counter. "He is way too competitive. So, what's shakin'?" The way she smiles at me almost makes me chicken out. When you're covered in mud, you don't want to touch anyone. "Chloe," she says, reaching across the counter and touching my chin. She presses her finger against my jawbone, turning my head slightly. Even with my knit hat pulled down low over my ears, I know she can see the edges of the bruise. She tilts her head, watching my eyes. "Todd? I'm taking my break." Todd pushes through the door smiling.

"Pressure's too much for you, is it?" He grabs another handful of cookies and funnels several chunks into his mouth. Raven doesn't turn away from me, her eyes keep watching me, pinning me there, so even if I wanted to run away, I can't. "You do realize that if you forfeit today, it's Lunchtime with Mussorgsky tomorrow, don't you?"

"Not now," she says, untying her apron. Todd stops chewing, watching her as she hangs her apron on the hook and reaches under the counter for her coat.

"So, I am to assume that you might not be taking just a fifteen-minute break today?"

"I'll be back," she says, zipping up the front of her coat. Todd frowns at her as she twists a gray and green scarf

Chloe

around her neck. "You ready?" she asks me, but I don't say anything, just nod. I'm not sure I'm ready for much of anything. Least of all this.

We drive for several minutes, taking a back way out of downtown and then a country road that I didn't even know existed. The back of Raven's car is filled with paper sacks, spilling over with balls of yarn in every color. They seem color coded. Green yarn in one. Yellow in another. Blue in another. "Sorry," she says, lifting a bag of orange yarn from the floor between my feet and shoving it into the back. She pokes the buttons on the stereo and Bananarama lamenting their cruel summer gives way to OMD promising that they won't let go at any price. "What color do you think Melon is?" She keeps watching the road, slowing around corners and straddling the potholes left by the snowplows.

"An orangish pink color?"

"Yeah, that's the accepted answer, but why?" Raven pushes one of the buttons again and the car is filled with U2 singing about a bloody Sunday. "I mean, what melon is that color? Not honeydew. Not crenshaw. Not even watermelon. Only cantaloupe. But is that, like, the melonest melon?" She slows the car down and takes a left down a dirt road, the rutted mud hard in the cold. "How about Sea Breeze or Peony or Elm? Or my personal favorite—Peppermint. Am I to assume that the sweater they are advertising is red and white striped?" I smile a little but feel the pressure on my cheek when I do. "You know what my dream is?"

"What?" I ask.

"I want to start a new line of yarn and name the colors things like Day Old Tuna and Frozen Pizza and Yellow Snow." I smile again. This time bigger.

"Or Moldy Cheddar," I say.

"Pencil Eraser."

"Dust Bunny."

"Potting Soil," she says, pulling the car even with a line of spruce trees and shutting it off. "And what about black and white? They don't mess with those. There's no Marshmallow or Midnight Sky."

"Is that what all of that is for?" I ask, looking into the back of the car.

"I make things," Raven says, pulling a bag from behind her onto her lap.

I stare through the windshield and across the blueberry barrens. I know the ocean is on the other side of the rocks, but the color of the water exactly matches the color of the sky, making it look as if the world simply stops, just runs out. Raven pulls a lump of red yarn free from the bag and hands it to me. "Here," she says. I lift the twist of yarn in my hands, letting my fingers sink into its softness, a scarf.

"It's beautiful," I say, opening up the weave and seeing the bits of glass winking at me.

"Sea glass," she says. "I found it all down there," she says, pointing at the nothingness on the other side of the field. I hold the scarf up to my cheek, feeling the cool touch of the glass and the softness of the yarn. I fold it carefully and try to hand it back to her, but she just puts up her hand. "Keep it," she says.

"Are you sure?" I ask. She just nods. I twist the scarf around my neck, feeling the scratchy warmth of the wool on my skin. I look back at Raven, but she's looking out the windshield.

"You don't have to tell me everything. I just want to know that you're safe."

"Safe," I say, and the word seems too big for the car. "Can we walk?" I ask, putting my hand on the door handle.

"As far as you want," Raven says. I open the door and climb out into the cold. We walk along the road in silence, listening to the crunch of snow under our shoes.

"Raven?" I push my hands deeper into my coat, trying to find some warmth hidden there. "Do you ever feel like nothing is how it was supposed to be? Like somehow everything got tossed into a big box and was shaken up until it was just one big mess?"

"Like a jigsaw puzzle."

"Yeah, but one with like a million pieces and no box top."

"I guess when my life feels like that, I just look for some familiar things. Some edge pieces."

"What if you can't find them?"

"You find someone to help you look." We keep walking, talking softly until we're too cold to continue. I tell her about last night, the weird Goth kids and how I made them laugh and then the drunk fishermen and how they hurt us. I tell her about Micah and the visitation. I start to tell her about Shana, but I can't quite find the words for that. Raven just nods, letting me talk until I'm finished. Then we head back. She starts the car and leans back, letting it warm up for a moment. "Just let me know if you want help," she says. She puts the car in gear and backs it up onto the road.

"I could use some makeup," I say, touching the side of my face.

"Ivory or porcelain?" she asks.

"Unbuttered Popcorn."

"Plain Yogurt."

"Cirrus Cloud." I smile as we bump back onto the main road. I lean my head against the glass, watching as the heat from my breath fogs the window. Even if the box keeps getting shaken up, maybe I can find a couple of pieces that fit together.

Chloe

CHAPTER TEN

Shana

FIRST THING THIS morning, Dad stood in the middle of the kitchen eating a piece of rye toast slathered with blackberry jam, and he stopped in midchew. "They'll be here in just a few hours, won't they?" he said, and I was thinking *please let that be a rhetorical question.* Because it would be just like him to totally space it, even though we've been getting ready for two days. Here is how bad he is—he noticed like a day late that Chlo had a black eye and that the corner of her lip was swollen, and she told him she ran into a door, which as excuses go is pretty much a giant blinking neon sign that says, I'M LYING. But he just nodded and told her to be more careful, and then maybe four hours later he noticed *my* black eye, almost a mirror image of Chlo's, plus the scratch that looks like someone tried to sandpaper my cheek, and I told him that I ran into a door, too. And I was in the mood to push it, pissed at him for being so obtuse. "The same door," I said. "We ran into opposite sides of it at the same time." But he wasn't listening, just his usual—disappearing down the rabbit hole of himself. He only nodded and mumbled something about having to fix that sometime.

I guess we're not much better than he is. I mean, all the rest of the morning Chlo and I have been straightening the place up, dusting everything and waxing the floors. It's probably lucky that they want to do the visit on a Saturday, when Chlo and I can be here. They always say that they want to observe the "family dynamic." For some reason when I hear that phrase I think of the old *Partridge Family* reruns, like we have a psychedelic bus and we sing. Instead we have a psycho mom, and we cry. Not very good for a sitcom, I guess. I pull a bunch of *National Geographics* out of the attic and artfully arrange them on the coffee table. Much better than the three-year-old *People* or *Sports Illustrated* issues we usually have. Chlo gets Micah to take a bath and put on clean clothes, and I straighten up everything. I can hear them in the back bedroom, practicing over and over the few words he knows in English—*hello, I am fine*. They never seem like real words from his mouth, more like just sounds his mouth makes. That's how it is with Mom, too, even when she's speaking in complete sentences. But I try not to think about it. That's the advice, isn't it? Try not to think about it. Soon that list of "its" will be so long I will have nothing left to think about at all. Dad is off somewhere while we work, probably in his office downstairs. After dusting and shining everything with lemon polish, I throw a tablecloth over the TV and put a vase of flowers on it, because I don't want them to think we're rotting his brain with cartoons. I can see them writing that on their clipboards: *noted—TV brain rot.* Then after a minute I take the vase and tablecloth away, because I don't want it to look like we're depriving him of anything. *Noted—no TV, cultural deprivation.* Then I turn it on, and two women are calling each other bitch and taking wild swings at each other while their clothes fall off and the screen goes fuzzy to cover them up. I put the tablecloth and vase back on top again.

Seeing those women makes me think about the guys who jumped us, and I stop cleaning to walk over to the oval mirror and look at my eye for about the hundredth time. Funny how it's called a "black eye," because it's anything but. The night of the fight we walked home almost without speaking, though Chlo kept asking me to slow down, and I couldn't, like maybe if I walked fast enough I could leave myself behind. And that's all I wanted—to be away from myself. Mom with her craziness, Dad with his distraction, even Chlo with her sea glass—everyone else found some path away from themselves, why couldn't I? Especially that night, when I couldn't stand myself, when I had to look back at Chlo and see the abrasions on her neck, her puffy eye, and know I'd done that to her? Stupid, stupid me. When we got to the house, finally, and I helped her take off the makeup, I couldn't even look at her, my hands still shaking. And the only thing she said was, "You have a gray eye," just whispering it, and I had no idea what she meant until I looked in my mirror and saw my black eye forming under all the white makeup, and it did look gray, just a hint of darkness. I thought of the Catholic kids we see walking home in their uniforms on Ash Wednesday, all of them with that gray smear of ash on their foreheads, like a wound they are proud of. I guess that's true of black eyes, too, but mine just made me look old, like half my face had turned forty while the rest stayed fifteen. When I see those Catholic kids, all I can think of is the crematorium in the back of the basement. Most people don't know that almost all the ashes they get in the urn are from the coffin, not the body. And nobody knows that Dad used to open the crematorium doors and turn on the burners to dry our clothes when they got wet outside in the snow. I look at my eye again now, the purple and yellow and red of it, and wonder what in the hell we are going to tell the social worker when she comes. I'm thinking the door story might not work so well this time.

And that's just what we need, something else to explain. I had to go to the mall to get air fresheners, the kind you plug in with the little built-in fan, because that's how paranoid we are—*if the house stinks, they might take Micah away.* I walked into the mall with my head down, making the mistake of going in the entrance by Chick-fil-A. That same guy

I knew but didn't stopped pouring lemonade long enough to lift his hand in a half-wave, but I didn't stop. I think he half-knew me, too. Half-knowing, half a wave. I didn't wave back. I got new towels for the bathroom, because our old ones were getting kinda ratty, and about three times people looked at me, slipped across this little expanse of silence, then popped the question: "What happened to you?" And that *is* the question. Like every time Dad gets a body in downstairs, he gets a certificate that he has to sign and send on to some state office, and at the very top is a line that says CAUSE OF DEATH, and I'm thinking maybe we all need another kind, one that says CAUSE OF LIFE. Tell us, in ten words or less, what happened to you, what happened to Chlo, to Dad, to Micah. Yeah, I guess Mom happened to us. But what happened to her? What happened to Vernon, to make him so lonely? What happened to Jason, to make his smile such a rarity? I got through it at the mall, though. Three questions, three answers. I told one lady I was a professional boxer and another that it was makeup for a movie I was starring in. And I told this jerk in Wal-Mart that someone asked me a rude question and so I kicked his sorry ass. That one was pretty funny, the look on the his face.

I hear a car door slam and run to the window for about the tenth time today. Not her, not yet, but already it's eleven o'clock and Dad is nowhere to be found. I yell down the steps and Vernon says he hasn't seen him, and I shut the kitchen door fast before Vernon has a chance to theorize about alien abduction or spontaneous combustion. So tired of this. So tired, and I just sit. Pull out the kitchen chair and put my chin on the table and do nothing more than look at my hands. Let them come, and when the lady with her too-much perfume and too-judgmental eyes comes walking in and wants to know what I'm doing, I will tell her. I'm looking at my hands.

Actually, I'm looking at my charm bracelet, the one that Mom split in half and gave to me and Chlo for her birthday. She said she got that from some book, the idea to give us stuff on her birthday. The bracelet split, then her mind split, then she split. Nice symmetry. When I turn my wrist, they make music, those little charms. I always wonder if it's half music, too, but I can't get my head around what that would sound like. My favorite one is the little open book with my name engraved on it in the teeniest letters, the last one she bought for me before she left. She got it after I wrote my own sci-fi novel in the eighth grade. It was fifty pages long and featured talking kitchen appliances that take over the world by refusing to let humans eat. The other charms are a little laptop computer, a sand dollar, a trolley car, a coffee cup. I look at all of them, spin the bracelet around my wrist, and then hear a spoon clatter to the floor. When I turn around, Micah is sitting on the floor in his good pants and his little button-down shirt, eating brown sugar out of the box. His face and clothes are smeared in wet brown sugar.

"Dammit, Chloe," I yell, jumping up to take the yellow box away from him. I snatch it away, and his face turns deep red, his Early Warning System for a bout of real crying, the loud, hard-to-breathe kind.

"What?" Chlo says as she turns the corner into the kitchen.

"*Look*," I say, unable to keep myself from looking again at her dark and puffy eye. Maybe we can punch Dad in the eye and tell them it's genetic. "Just look at him, Chlo. Look at the floor, which I cleaned about fifteen minutes ago."

"Look at this, look at that. You should be a tour guide."

"You're supposed to be *watching* him, getting him ready." I grab the dustpan and start sweeping, but most of the sugar is stuck to the floor where he got his hands in it. Micah starts crying so hard that a string of spit drips out of his mouth. God. Chloe kneels down to hold him and looks up at me.

"Nice job," she says. "And I did get him ready. I told him to come stay with Dad while I cleaned up my room."

"Any particular dad?" I bend down to sponge the sugar off the floor. "Because ours isn't around."

She blinks and looks around the kitchen, as if he might be standing right there. "Well," she says, "where is he?"

"I don't know. You know, we really can't keep misplacing parents like this all the time."

"Don't . . ." She flushes, the scrapes on her neck going dark red.

"We need to get that crap on our faces soon," I tell her.

When I was at the mall I bought some makeup that was supposed to cover up anything, including scars and tattoos. Now if they just made an emotional version of that, we'd be all set.

"I know," Chloe says. "What time is it?"

And like an answer to her question, there is a knock on the door. The side door, with the wooden step up from the sidewalk. Chlo and I look at each other. Micah has stopped crying, but his face looks like a road map, all flushed and tearstained. The floor is brown and sticky. Dad is missing in action.

And just like that, the social worker is at our door.

All smiles, and *sorry I'm late* when she's early, and the clipboard is in her hands, and she wears on the lapel of her jacket a button that says, HELPING IS OUR MIDDLE NAME. So, what's the first name, I wonder, NOT? She answers that thought by introducing herself as Ms. Ballentine, which I hear as Ms. Valentine until she hands me her card. I stand there like a retarded mannequin while she walks in, and thank god Chloe steps up, offering her some coffee she thought to make. This woman has serious hair and those fake blue contact lenses that make your eyes look chlorinated. I see her looking at both of *our* eyes, then trying not to look, then looking. My brain digs around for an excuse, and I'm thinking the ones I used at the mall probably won't fly.

"Well, Micah," she says, bending forward like he's

fallen into a well or something. "How is my little man?" Now I'm picturing a midget in a well, and it's all I can do not to laugh. Nervous, nervous me. She glances at Chlo, really takes a long, hard look at her eye, and I'm thinking *just ask us already*, even though I've got nothing if she does. The question hangs in the air like an unexploded hand grenade.

Micah says, "Hello, I am fine," and he says it the way a parrot would, but we all laugh anyway like it's the cutest thing in the universe. Ms. Ballentine uses her thumb to wipe at the dried smear of brown sugar on his cheek, then writes some stuff on her clipboard while I stand there trying to imagine what—*Note: Child has been caramelized.* Then she walks around the kitchen while she's asking us about the weather and stuff, like she's just some friendly person from an elevator who happened to walk into our house. She stops and looks at the collection of cookbooks—Mom's—still crowding the shelves. She turns her head to the side to read the titles, and I can't figure it out. I mean, is it like if we have the right cookbooks then Micah is getting the proper nutrition? Chlo glances at me and gives a little shrug.

"So, who's the cook?" she says. She turns to me and smiles, holding the clipboard against her, tapping her chest with it.

"Our—" Chloe begins.

"Me," I say quickly. "I cook all the time. Like just last week I made a baked Alaska." Actually, I have no idea what that even is, but I remember some movie where a bunch of rich people ordered it in a fancy restaurant.

"Did you now?" She smiles in a slight way that makes me want to punch her in the face. Then she writes something down. "Where is your father?"

"Out," I say. "I mean, he went down to the store. He'll be back any second."

She nods. "And is he often out when you are here alone?"

"I'm fifteen," I say. "I'm certified as a babysitter." This last part isn't true, though I once did think about taking a course at the Y.

She nods again, and I imagine that in social worker school there was a whole unit on meaningful nodding. "You understand that Micah has very special needs. He requires a stable environment, not a babysitter."

"Our father isn't *missing*," Chloe says, her face red. "He went down to the store to buy stuff to make pancake batter. He makes us pancakes every Saturday. It's cool, Ms. Ballentine. He drizzles the batter around and makes them shaped like flowers and Mickey Mouse and peace symbols."

She raises her eyebrows, clearly impressed. And it would be impressive if she had a time machine and could go back a year and a half or so, when Dad really *did* do that for us, every Saturday morning, while Mom painted. Mostly now, we just get our own breakfasts, usually cereal or chocolate milk.

"Well," she says, "that's very impressive. You girls are

very lucky to have that. My own father's specialty is chili, but it doesn't make for a very good breakfast." We both laugh like it's the best joke we ever heard, and even Micah laughs, just because we are.

Ms. Ballentine tucks her pen behind her ear, like we are all done here, and I start to breathe again. It's probably just a routine-visit kind of thing, like they just want to make sure we don't have rats or aren't lying around shooting up heroin or something. Routine. We pass.

"So," Ms. Ballentine says, hugging her clipboard to her chest, "how did you girls get those black eyes? The scratches?" She looks from one of us to the other. Micah laughs again, like he still thinks her lame chili joke is funny, but his laugh is the only sound in the room. When we don't say anything, she shrugs, raises her eyebrows. "Well," she says, "were you fighting?"

"Yes," I say. "We were fighting."

"Shana . . ." Chloe says.

"With one another?" she says.

"God, no," I say. "With fishermen."

She takes a breath, but I don't care. Let her take a million goddamn breaths. "Do you mind telling me why you were fighting with fishermen?"

Chloe looks at me like I just pulled a gun on Ms. Ballentine.

"Because we both really, really hate fish," I say. Ms. Ballentine looks at Chloe and even at Micah, like they might be able to explain this. "That was just a joke, Ms. Ballentine," I say. "Like your chili thing before."

"I see. That still doesn't explain—"

"They jumped us," I tell her. "We were walking through Old Port, headed to Big Mama's for a milkshake, and they just jumped us and started hitting us."

She frowns. "For no reason."

"Yes, for no reason. Or the reason that they're stupid rednecks and we aren't. You should be at *their* houses, checking on *their* kids."

She nods again. Nod, nod—she's a pro. "I have another appointment. When will your father be home?"

"I don't know," I say.

"He did realize his appointment was this morning?"

"He must've been delayed," Chloe says. "Or maybe he couldn't find some ingredient or something."

Even Chloe can hear how lame that sounds. Ms. Ballentine brings the clipboard down and practically starts writing a novel on it. She talks and writes at the same time, telling us that we should give her card to our father, that she will have to plan another visit sooner than the schedule would dictate, that there may be surprise follow-ups. That makes it sound like some kind of party, I'm thinking, with hats and balloons and streamers. Then again, I have had enough surprises for one year. Finally Ms. Ballentine and her important hair and her phony lapel button leave, and we are left standing in the silence, in that neatened-up room with *National Geographic*s and no TV. Chloe silently follows me back into the kitchen and looks out the window at nothing. I take the yellow box of brown sugar from the kitchen table and hand it to Micah, who's sitting in the corner by the refrigerator, where the warm air blows out. "Here you go," I say to him. "Knock yourself out."

CHAPTER ELEVEN

Chloe

"WHO WOULD WIN? A polar bear, or a thousand bees?" Todd asks, lifting the drawer out of the cash register.

"Bees," Raven says, pressing the khaki-colored napkins into the silver holder. She holds up a napkin and reads from it. "'Made with seventy-five percent post-consumer waste.' Not really the thing you want to be wiping your mouth with, is it?" I shake my head and keep wiping the top of the glass display case.

"You can't just say bees," Todd says, stacking the money from the drawer into neat piles. Raven rolls her eyes at me and smiles. This has become my nightly ritual. Help get Micah into bed (or not), walk down here, and work behind the counter during the nightly postmovie, postdinner, preparty, prestudying rush. *Anyone asks, you're sixteen*, Todd told me the first night. At first I felt bad about leaving Micah with Shana, felt like I was taking advantage of her, but then I thought *Why?* Half the time Micah's with Vernon anyway, plus I doubt she ever felt guilty about leaving me to take care of things while she got away. "Okay, Chloe, your turn." I turn and take a bite out of my blueberry scone and lean my hip against the counter, chewing and thinking.

"Superman or Batman?" I ask.

"Superman Red or Superman Blue?" Todd asks, tapping the edge of one stack of twenties on the counter before snapping a rubber band around it.

"Either one," I say. I look over at Raven, who just shrugs.

"Okay, let's say Superman Red, because he's the one most people are familiar with."

"So your answer is Superman?" Raven asks.

"Duh," Todd says, going back to his counting.

"Why duh?" Raven asks. She doesn't look up from the funnel she is holding over the cinnamon shakers.

"Superman has about seventeen major super powers." Todd stops stacking and turns to face us. "Flying, heat vision, super speed, super strength, freezing breath." He ticks off each one, holding up his other hand when he runs out of fingers. "X-ray vision, impenetrable skin, dimensional teleportation, electron manipulation."

"Okay there, Superdork, I think we have a pretty good idea." Raven smiles as she says it, but Todd just squints at her. "I'm going to go with Batman," she says. She places the funnel over another shaker and begins pouring nutmeg into it. Todd makes a noise that sounds like a faucet being turned on after a really cold night. "Batman has a gadget for everything. The batarang, the batcopter, the batmobile, the batapult. . . ."

"Not to mention all of the things in his utility belt," I say.

"And the Bat Cave," she says, waggling her eyebrows at me. Todd squints at her again.

"The category is which is more likely to win in a fight, not which one you would be more likely to date," he says.

"I know," Raven says, making her eyes go soft. "But he is dreamy." She looks over at me and smiles vacantly, making me crack up.

"You just like him because he's all dark and mysterious," Todd says. I'm aware that somehow we aren't talking about Superman and Batman anymore.

"Actually," Raven says, pushing open the door to the back room with her hip, her hands full of huge jugs of cinnamon, nutmeg, and cocoa powder, "I like him because he's smart. Really smart." She lets the door *whoosh* shut behind her. I take another bite of my scone before dropping the rest of it into the trash can. I see Todd's cheeks turning pink, then his ears, then his neck, as if he is slowly turning pink one body part at a time. The door bumps again, swinging outward this time with Raven right behind it. "All right then, Chloe, you ready to go home?" she asks. I nod and put my plate into the empty busing basin beneath the counter. I notice my hand is shaking as I let go of the plate. Home, I think. A place that should be comforting, but somehow is just the opposite.

"See you, Chloe," Todd says, following us to the door, keys in hand to lock it behind us. "Raven," he says, but his voice cracks a bit in the middle so it comes out more like "Rain." She smiles at him and the pink starts up again.

"'Night, Todd," she says. We both push our hands into our pockets and our faces down into our collars to block the wind as we walk to where her car sits, its tires half buried in the snow deposited by the plows.

"You don't have to give me a ride," I say, pulling open the passenger-side door. The cold vinyl pops and cracks under me as I slide into the seat. "It's only a couple of blocks."

"You're not walking home alone," Raven says, pushing her key into the ignition and pumping the gas pedal once. The engine sputters twice and threatens not to start. Raven stops and pats the dashboard. "Come on," she whispers. On the third try it rumbles to life, and cold air blasts at us from the vents. "Sorry," she says, sliding the heater button to off. We sit for a moment, staring through the frosted windshield and watching as the defroster slowly begins to work, clearing the lowest part of the window first.

"I think Todd likes you," I say.

"Yeah," she says, so softly I have to look right at her to hear the rest. "He does." But the way she says it sounds sad, almost regretful.

"He's nice," I offer. "And smart." She just nods. "And cute," I say. I see a smile playing at the corner of her mouth for a moment, but then it disappears, making me think it was just the lights playing a trick on me.

"He's great," she says quietly. I keep watching her, waiting for more, but there isn't any. She brushes her mittened hand against the inside of the windshield, clearing some of the frost that is clinging there. "Guess we'd better get you home," she says, smiling over at me, but her smile is thin, as if it can't quite stretch to cover the thing it's supposed to be covering. She releases the emergency brake and lets the car roll back a bit before shifting and pulling out onto the street. We ride silently, hearing the rumble of the tires over the cobblestones and the crunch of ice as she pulls across the plow lines in front of my building. "Sometimes what you can't see is more real than what you can," she says, rubbing her thumb across the steering wheel.

"How so?" I ask, watching the way the light fractures in the windshield as the headlights of passing cars play over us.

"Maybe it's because when you don't think anyone can see something, you don't try to hide it. I mean, it's there, but it's invisible."

"Invisible."

"No," she says. "That's not quite right. I don't know. It's hard to explain. Maybe it's just that you push all the other stuff to the front, the stuff that you know people want to see. The stuff that people understand. Then the other stuff, the really scary or strange or complicated stuff . . . you just leave that in the back. I mean, it's there. There if someone wanted to see it, but it's hidden." I look back over at her, and she gives me this half smile. "I'm not making much sense," she says.

I push my chin back down into my scarf, where my warm breath stays locked against me, filling my nose with the scent of blueberry and coffee and peppermint gum. I start to try and think of what she's hiding in plain sight. And you just can't ask. I try to guess at it, but realize there's no way. I mean, who would guess my secret? Who would guess that a somewhat average-looking fourteen-year-old with a hand-me-down winter coat and a new red scarf would have a mother who I remember now more from photographs than real life? I look up at Raven. "You are making sense. Perfect sense," I say, even if it isn't exactly the truth. We keep sitting there until the heater finally warms up and the glass clears and our breath stops making clouds around our faces.

"He *is* cute though, isn't he?" Raven finally says. She smiles over at me, making me laugh.

"And smart."

"And funny."

"And nice."

"And he seems to know a lot about superheroes," she says, making us both laugh again, and somewhere in the laughing I feel it. A tiny bit of the pressure being let off, making it just a bit easier to breathe.

On the day Ms. Ballentine visited, Dad did finally come home a little after noon—almost half an hour after she left and almost a full hour after the scheduled appointment. When he walked in, Micah was still sitting on the floor of the kitchen, spoon in his hand, his head resting against the cabinet behind him. I was sitting in the chair facing the fireplace, pretending to read the book in my lap. When we heard the key push into the lock, Shana came out of the back, walking hard, her boots thunking on the wooden floor. "Finally," she said under her breath. He walked into the entryway, unzipping his coat, shifting a bag from one hand to the other. A plastic bag, MARTEN'S written across the side in blue block lettering. For an instant I thought maybe Shana had been right. Maybe he had just been down at the store, buying eggs and pancake mix and cinnamon and vanilla. Maybe the cash register had stopped working or there was a line or he got stuck behind someone trying to sneak thirteen items into the ten-or-less lane. I could see that Shana had the same thought, too, because suddenly all of the anger dropped from her face. Then we both realized the truth at the same moment. We saw that the bag was way too small for syrup and milk and pancake stuff. There was only one thing in the bag, and it was long and rectangular. A carton of cigarettes. We both looked at him, waiting, and I could see Micah lean forward, lifting his head. And Dad just stood there, with his coat half unzipped. "Sorry, girls," he said and he walked between us through the apartment without even looking at Micah. He went to the living room window and pushed it open and climbed out onto the roof. He paused for a moment to zip his coat back up before turning and pushing the window closed behind him.

"Sorry?" Shana said loudly. It was the first loud thing that we had heard since Ms. Ballentine had left, pulling the door shut hard behind her. "You're sorry?" she said again, this time even louder. I could still see him through the window, his shoulders pulled up against the cold, against our looks, and now against Shana's anger.

"Shana, don't," I said softly.

"Why the hell not?" she asked, and I didn't know what to say. I just shook my head. I mean, what's the point? Anger would only push him further away. We could hear the screech of the metal chair legs against the asphalt roof as he pulled it forward into a tiny patch of sunlight. We knew he would sit there for hours, lighting each cigarette with the one before it, stringing them together, as if giving himself something to hold on to. We knew he'd plant the spent butts in the flowerpot that used to hold daisies and pansies and snapdragons. He'd push them deep into the soil, nestling them against the hundreds of others there. Planting a crop of sadness and sickness and longing. Waiting to see what might grow out of it. Nothing we would want to stick in a vase and look at during dinner. Shana turned and clunked to the back of the apartment again, her anger so hot I could almost feel it.

"Chlo-ee," Micah said softly from the kitchen. "I'm cold."

"Me, too," I said, pushing myself to standing and walking over to where he was still sitting. "Come on," I said, reaching down for him. "Let's go get you cleaned up."

That was two weeks ago. And we keep waiting for a surprise visit. Keep waiting to hear the rap of official knuckles on our door. It's like a pop quiz that you know is coming but you don't know how to study for. And all I can think is that if we couldn't manage to pass the take-home-open-book test, I can't see how we are going to pass a surprise quiz, one that we don't have answers to. One that we don't even know how to begin to study for.

I look over at Micah, curled into one of the purple chairs near the front windows. I'm pretty sure he's asleep, but it's hard to tell from where I'm standing. After the visit, I just can't manage to stay in the apartment for more than a few minutes at a time, finding any excuse to get out. I notice that Shana is doing the same, spending most of her time downstairs helping Vernon. Dad isn't any better, spending most of his time locked in his office downstairs and the rest huddled on the roof, smoking cigarette after cigarette. I remember Shana telling me that Marlboros are about the worst cigarette there is. *If smoking a regular cigarette is like poking holes in your lungs with a stick, smoking one of those unfiltered things is like taking your whole respiratory system out and beating the crap out of it with a baseball bat.* I guess if I were a good daughter I'd be bugging him to quit, but it seems like just one more thing on the big pile of things to worry about, and sometimes it feels like that pile is going to just come down on top of me and bury me.

The first night I didn't have a real plan, I just sort of left. Shana was standing in the entryway with her boots in her hand and her scarf tied around her neck, and I just walked past her and through the front door, leaving her to deal with Dad and Micah and whatever else might happen. I just sort of drifted around downtown (not one of my best plans) and finally settled on sitting between the stacks at the library. Knees pulled in so that I could pull my coat down over them. A book balancing on top of my knees. *The Annotated Brothers Grimm.* Not really reading it, just feeling the weight of it on my legs.

The second night Shana was waiting for me.

"Where are you going?" she asked, and while I didn't actually have an answer I told her it was none of her business. "When will you be back?" she asked. I gave her the same answer. I thought I'd won until she pushed past me and out the door, telling me that Dad was in the studio and that Micah needed someone to read to him. I thought about just following her out, leaving everything behind me. No more responsibility. No more long nights listening to my father crying and Micah calling out. No more staring at the sea glass or shuffling through old paintings, trying to find answers to anything, everything, just one thing. But Micah kept me tethered there. I realized that with Dad almost a ghost and Shana so angry that she seemed almost to shine with it, I was all that was left. Instead of taking my coat off, pulling my boots from my feet, I went into Micah's room and told him to get dressed.

"Wear something warm," I told him. "We're going out." I almost stopped when instead of asking *why* or *where* he just got out of bed and went to his closet and pulled out his gray hoodie and a pair of jeans. What was it that drove the questions from his mind? Trust, or fear? I waited in the hallway, holding his blue fleece jacket, the one with rocket ships and planets and aliens all over it. "You ready?" I asked him. I helped him push his arms into the coat, held the bottom of the zipper while he pulled the metal rocket ship up to his throat. I needed a destination that night. Somewhere warm. Somewhere safe. Somewhere that we could just be for a while. I held his mittened hand, making the journey that we had made before, walking down the street dodging the puddles and up to the coffeehouse door.

Todd sometimes lets Micah help out after it slows down. *If anyone asks, you're sixteen*, he deadpans. Micah just nods solemnly each time, using the tamper to pack grounds into the espresso filter. For his help, he gets to choose anything in the case that he wants. He always takes a long time deciding, even though the choices are always the same. Then he always chooses the same thing: ginger cookie. But the way he says it, it sounds exotic. He takes his cookie and his milk to one of the purple chairs and watches the balls of lights in the trees across the street twinkle while he eats. When it's time to go, I usually find him curled up in the chair asleep, cookie crumbs clinging to his cheeks, a milk mustache above his mouth.

"Taste this," Raven says, pushing a cup filled with something pink toward me.

"What is it?"

"Don't," Raven says, lifting her palm toward Todd when he tries to tell me. "Just one sip." I lift the cup and sniff it, but all I smell is sweet. "Just one taste." I put my lips to the edge of the cup and slowly tilt it toward my mouth, feeling the smooth heat against my lips and then my tongue. Then mint. It's as if my whole mouth explodes. I put the cup back on the counter and try to figure out what to do with the pink stuff that is still sitting on my tongue. "Go ahead," Raven says, pointing to the sink. I lean into the basin and open my mouth, letting it fall from me like a pink waterfall. "See, I told you," Raven says behind me. "It's gross."

"What is it?" I ask after rinsing my mouth out with water twice. I can still taste the minty syrup coating the insides of my cheeks.

"It's called a Mintuccino," Todd says, pouring the rest

of it down the drain. "It's supposed to replace the eggnog thing from last year."

"The Eggnogaccino," Raven says, trying not to laugh. "It was pretty bad, too, but at least it wasn't pink with red sprinkles."

"It's supposed to be festive," Todd says, but he's smiling now, too. "The good news is that we are going to be serving them up, starting the day after Thanksgiving."

"No, the good news is that the holidays are almost here," Raven says. I shrug and look over at Todd, who is just standing there, staring at her. "What's wrong with you two? Christmas? Big holiday. Tree, lights, presents? Fat guy in a red suit?"

"I'm not that into Christmas," I say, thinking about last year and how Dad almost forgot all about it.

"Me neither," Todd says. Raven just stares at us, looking back and forth like she's doing one of those *circle the things that are wrong in each picture* puzzles.

"Well," she says, "prepare to be into it this year. Prepare to be into it up to your eyeballs. Prepare to be drenched in it. Because I love Christmas."

Todd smiles at me. "Bring it on," he says.

"As long as it doesn't involve any more of that," I say, pointing to the cup on the counter still dripping pink goo.

"No, this Christmas is going to be the best one ever," Raven says. I keep thinking about that while Raven gives Micah and me a ride home and as I am tucking him into bed and as I curl up under my covers and stare through the glass on my shelves. Green and red lights wink back at me as the sea glass catches the passing headlights and the stray bits of moonlight sliding in my window. *"The best one ever,"* I whisper to myself. I whisper something else right after. Something to ward off any bad luck or bad karma or just plain bad. Something that might sound something like a prayer to someone, but that sounds only like the tiniest breath of air as I fall asleep. *Please.*

CHAPTER TWELVE

Shana

WHY NOT START the day with a few random acts of destruction?

Two weeks now, and still no surprise visit, no report on
the observation, and I've had it. Every knock on the door,
every voice from the TV—it's like we're haunted by something that hasn't happened yet. I mean, it's almost Thanksgiving, which means another visit to see Mom, and I am
waiting for Dad to start bringing home new bottles of Old
Crow to go with his boxes of Marlboros, and I want to tell
him not to be such a stupid cliché about all of it. If you're
going to fall apart, at least be original. Drop-in visit, go see
Mom, wait for Dad to take his drinks to the roof—it's like
we're a movie and someone clicked the pause button right
before something bad was about to happen. I'm at the end,
tired to death of it. Last night, at maybe two in the morning, a candlestick fell out of its holder because Chloe forgot

to stick it in with clay, and I ran out to the front hall, convinced that it was time for our surprise visit, in the middle of the night.

So as soon as Dad does his morning disappearing act and Chloe heads off to day care with Micah, I call in sick to the high school. They tell me that I have to have a parent call, and I'm like, what's the deal? I thought they were supposed to be preparing us for the real world, and someone correct me if I'm wrong, but I'm pretty sure that in the real world you call in sick to work yourself and don't need your mom to do it for you. So anyway, I wait ten minutes then call back and say I am my mother and don't even bother disguising my voice. Then I go into the study, find Dad's carton of cigs on top of the printer, and I take them to the back door, out on the landing. I start pitching those red packs, one at a time, out into the alley, throwing them as far as I can, so that half of them land on the roof of the building across the alley from us. Then I just start throwing them anywhere, throwing them away, spinning them out red and white against the sky. Manna from heaven, that is, if God wanted to kill everyone, and I think he pretty much does, right? That's why people keep dying. After the cigs are all gone, I go into the kitchen and dig in the cabinets above the stove and find the few bottles we have, one with about an inch of bourbon in it, and a bottle of red wine, and even the bottle of cooking sherry that Mom used to keep there.

I smash them all, right down in the middle of the alley, the smell of it finding me even so high up.

And then I go back into Chloe's room and there it is, leaning against the wall by her bed—the last painting Mom did before losing her mind, the one with the angel at the end of the alley, hanged and bleeding on a chain-link fence. She sits in here, Chloe, staring at it, seeing it as beautiful in the way some people always see sad things as beautiful. So sad and beautiful, all of us. Yeah, right. Put us on the list with rainy days and old people and Jesus. Let's all write romantic songs about suicide. A beautiful death? I don't think so. I think I'll take the mall instead, all that plastic and fluorescence and happy, happy music, insisting on a life that is no more complicated than an Orange Julius and a NASCAR clock. Shallow me out, God. There's a prayer for you. That's why nothing's real, because the one big real thing is death and we burn up our lives trying not to think about it, because if you think about it you turn into Mom, and already I can't sleep at night because I worry that's Chloe. My little Chloe, sitting in here staring at that painting, falling into all that sad and beautiful death and slowly slipping away from me, slowly turning into Mom. Well, no. No.

In the kitchen I yank open the drawers until I find the razor knife that Mom used to trim the linoleum when we first moved in, and five seconds later I am back in Chloe's room cutting the painting out of its frame. Four slices, all done, the frame left behind like dried bones, and then I start razoring the painting itself, slicing it into long strips, and flecks of paint break off and dot Chloe's bed, falling in the colored light, the long strips sliced into pieces, the pieces into bits, and at some point I have sliced the webbing on my thumb and am bleeding, smears of it on the inside of my arm, and for half a second I think it's coming from the painting itself, from wet paint that somehow never dried. When I finish that I gather up all the pieces and take them out onto the landing and scatter them to the wind, then tip the frame off over the railing, watch it fall three stories to the alley below and break into sticks of pale pine.

Chloe will hate me. But I don't care; let her. She's never been to the hospital, doesn't know how bad Mom is. If she did, maybe she would stop saying things like . . . *when Mom comes back we can all* . . . she isn't coming back. Not to here, not to herself. Like during services downstairs, you hear people telling each other that whoever has gone to a better place. It's like that, only she's gone and it's not really anyplace, gone into nothing. A few good breezes and that stupid painting will be gone into nothing, too. And then maybe Chloe will get it, stop romanticizing the damage. But no, she probably won't. Not until she sees. And that's it, I think. Chloe needs to go with us. Chloe needs to see.

+ + +

Since I'm out sick and not really sick, I spend the afternoon with Vernon, just helping him downstairs. Once a year he shampoos the carpet in the chapel and gets up on a ladder to dust and wash the chandelier. I have chandelier duty. Vernon moves up the middle of the aisle behind that big, noisy machine, pushing it along, the big sponges beneath it moving in slow, soapy circles. Today Vernon is wearing suspenders and has his shirt buttoned all the way up, which makes him look like he ought to be playing checkers in a calendar painting somewhere. I have to polish each of the little glass baubles hanging down from the lamp, and there's about a million of them. I keep thinking about the pile of stuff just on the other side of the far wall, the alley full of wood and broken bottles and crumpled packs of cigarettes, like a convenience store committed suicide. That's funny, and I half-smile to myself, if only not to think about how pissed everyone will be at me when they get home.

Vernon shuts off the machine and leans against it, breathing heavily. "How come 'fat chance' and 'slim chance' mean the same thing?" he says. "And how come you aren't in school?"

I drop my sponge back into the bucket of suds. "You really want to know?"

"Of course."

"Well, I think it's just one of those quirks of the English language. There's no real explanation."

He grins. "I meant school."

"I know."

"Maybe they expelled you for fighting."

I roll my eyes. "Vernon, I have told you a hundred times, we got attacked. I didn't fight anyone."

"Uh-huh. Two to tango," he says, except that he starts the machine again as he says it and I miss the last part. I know what he says, though, because he says it every day.

I go back to the chandelier, my arms tired and heavy from working overhead. I keep thinking about wanting to get out of here, especially after Dad and Chlo get home, but I don't know where to go. I haven't Goth'd up and headed to the port since that night, even though Jason and Magenta and some of the others keep e-mailing me and leaving me messages, wondering where I am. It's a good question, because I don't know where I am, really.

Vernon shuts the machine down, halfway up the aisle. "What if there were no more hypothetical questions?" he says, then adjusts his suspenders again.

"So, the machine is part of your act now?"

He pats the red handles. "Could be. Maybe shutting off the irritating noise will improve people's appreciation for my witticisms."

"I'm confused. The machine or your witticisms are the irritating noise?"

"What a smart-ass you turned out to be," he says, smiling. "We had such high hopes for you."

He's still smiling and so am I, but something about this last line lands wrong, and he suddenly blushes deeply, then pretends to mess with the controls on the machine. He starts it up again, and I notice how much he's sweating, his brown shirt darker in spots. We fall back into the work, Vernon shampooing while I clean. I notice at the edges of my fingernails little flecks of black polish, a little bit of Goth still clinging to me. I do miss them, Jason and Magenta especially, despite how screwed up they are. I mean, so what? Who isn't? Vernon shuts down the machine again and I automatically drop my sponge in the bucket, waiting for the next one-liner.

"Yeah?" I say, smiling.

He isn't. "Your father is going to run this place into the ground," he says. He's nervous, patting his mouth with his hand. "I mean, he could go to jail."

My stomach freezes, exactly like it did at the moment I realized that those fishermen were coming after us. "What do you mean?" I say, stepping down from the ladder. "Why?"

Vernon tugs his suspenders. "Neglect. People come in here and do a prepay, and he's not opening the accounts. He puts their check in the safe."

I shrug. "I thought checks belonged in a safe. And what's a prepay?"

"Checks belong in the bank. People come in and pay for the whole funeral way ahead of time, twenty years maybe.

That money earns interest, and then when the time comes, the whole deal is all paid for, and they don't have to bother making any arrangements."

"So, take it out of the safe and put it in the bank."

He shakes his head. "Some of it he's cashed out. Some of the checks have expired. There's no accounting, is what I'm trying to say. For a business, that means trouble."

I nod, but Vernon's words remind me of the way we've been teaching English to Micah, with me telling him the English word, then Chloe saying *that means* . . . and giving him the equivalent word in Russian, using the same phrase, *that means . . . that means. Water, apple, coat, toy* . . . the one word we didn't teach him was *trouble*. And it's probably the one we should have started with.

The mall has become my white makeup. I disappear here, walk through as just another girl with dark hair and jeans, hidden in plain sight. Sometimes here I just walk around in circles, heading down all the little chutes like a pinball, walking laps and laps, like one of the old people who come there every morning. Right now the mall workers are busy putting together Santa's Fantasy Land, which features a train that runs around a little track, plus a fake road sign that says NORTH POLE, and a camera so they can sell pictures to all the parents. Last year they had "pet day," and all these grown-up people came with their dogs and cats and sat on

Santa's lap themselves, holding the pet, smiling for a photo. On a dare from Magenta I got a cup of water from Arby's and told the elf-girls that the water contained my pet sea monkeys, and they had no choice but to let me pose with Santa, my face painted white and black, while I held up a cup of tap water.

I make a lap past the Nail Shack, past the Hairport, the Gap, Plan-9 Arcade, Beary Christmas, Hickory Farm, Hats in the Belfry, and then turn the corner toward the food court, pass by Chick-fil-A, and there he is again, and again he's at the lemonade in his paper hat. I wonder briefly if they start you on lemonade and slowly move you up to chicken, some odd evolution at work. Then, like we are following the same script every week, I walk past and kinda half-look, and he kinda half-looks, and I wonder again who the hell he is, and I get the half-wave.

Enough halves. I walk over, around the people standing in line, right up next to the lemonade dispenser. Whoever he is, he's wearing an EMPLOYEE OF THE MONTH badge on his smock.

"Okay," I say. "Who are you?"

He puts a plastic lid on a cup before he looks up again. "Hi, Shana," he says, and if I didn't know his face, I know his voice.

It's Jason.

"No *way*," I say, so loudly that people in line turn to look at me. White paper hat instead of white makeup, red smock instead of all that black. But sure enough, it's him.

"Way," he says, smiling now, handsome now. Really, he looks like Clark Kent or something, except no glasses and less dorky. And I can see the six holes in his left ear, even though he's not wearing any earrings.

"How did you know it was me?" I ask him. "I didn't know it was you until I heard your voice. I know that voice."

"Your walk. I know that walk," he says.

"My walk?"

He *shusshes* another lemonade into another foam cup. "You lope," he says.

I feel my face warm. "Thanks so much," I say. "I was running a little low on self-consciousness today."

"No, no," he says. When he shakes his head, the paper hat moves around. "It's hot. Trust me."

"I have a hot lope?"

He twists his mouth, frowns a little. "Sounds a little strange when you put it that way. But yeah, you do."

"Well, thanks." I look at him again, thinking how the white makeup always makes his eyes look yellowed and muddy, but now they are not that way at all. They are clear and dark, dark brown, almost-but-not-quite black. Oreo-cookie color.

"I'm done here," he says. "You want to go somewhere?"

"How do you know when you've poured enough lemon-ades for one day?"

He shakes his head. "If you have to ask the question, you'll never be the lemonade guy."

"Another shattered dream," I say, one of those awkward things I sometimes forget and say around the wrong people, but right now it doesn't feel awkward. It feels like I'm having fun.

CHAPTER THIRTEEN

Chloe

I DIDN'T NOTICE it was missing. Not for a while at least. Not until I was nearly asleep, just barely listening to the sounds of the plows trying to stay ahead of the snowstorm. It was like I had to almost tip over into sleep before I realized something was different. Something was gone. Maybe that's how it always is with things disappearing. It isn't until you relax a bit, let yourself breathe, shut your eyes that you realize something isn't right. It wasn't like when someone realizes something in a movie. They sit up fast and click on the light and stare wildly at the camera or almost the camera and the audience gasps *Oh no!* or sighs *Finally!* I just lay there with my eyes still shut, feeling my fingers curl in toward my palms until I could feel the half-moons of pain where my nails dug into my skin. *The painting.*

I went into Micah's room first, quietly stepping past his bed toward the closet. I stepped inside and pulled the door mostly closed behind me before pulling the chain attached to the bare lightbulb. It took a moment for my eyes to adjust to the bright light and more than a moment for my eyes to adjust to what they were seeing. His clothes were piled on the floor at my feet, some folded, some not. Bare hangers were pushed to the far sides of the rod to make room for the boxes, maybe twenty of them. Stacked one on top of the other, crowding the shelves, covering the wood floor. I pushed the one closest to me with my toe, but it wouldn't budge. I pushed harder, mashing the cardboard in a bit on the side, but the box still didn't move. I bent and pulled at the flaps. The box was filled nearly to the top with stones, all nearly the same size and shape—flat and rounded. Perfect skipping rocks. The box next to it was filled with wadded up balls of aluminum foil. The third with a rainbow of twist ties from the necks of bread bags. A fourth seemed empty until I looked more closely. There in the corner was my piece of red sea glass. I pulled the chain above my head and backed out of the closet, looking toward the bed as my eyes adjusted once again to the darkness. Even in the dark and even under half a dozen blankets I could see Micah breathing. I watched the mound in the middle of the bed rise slightly then fall again, each breath slow and rhythmic.

A thin line of light shone beneath the door leading downstairs. Another under Shana's door. Still another under my father's bedroom door. Only darkness crept out from under

the last door. The only place the painting could be. Someone had put it back in there. Back with the others. Maybe
Shana, maybe my father. Behind the door they both knew I
would never go through. I placed my hand against the door,
feeling the cold, slick surface of the painted wood. I leaned
my forehead against it and closed my eyes. As I reached
down for the doorknob, my charm bracelet slid down my
wrist and the bits of silver clinked against each other as
they rested against my hand. I turned the knob slowly all
the way to the right before pulling it toward me. Another
breath. Then another. Then two more. "The painting," I
whispered to myself. And then I pushed.

It was bad at the end. Really bad. It was like we were all eating dinner, eating the same awful soup. Too salty. Too spicy.
Too hot. Spoonful after spoonful. Trying not to actually
make eye contact with one another. It was as if we were all
sitting in a theater, popcorn clutched in our hands, watching a really bad movie. One that keeps getting worse. The
plot unraveling. Bad acting, bad music. Everything pulling
apart, but we kept sitting there, watching it, holding our
breath, thinking *Maybe it's just me. Maybe it isn't as bad as I
think it is.* But from this side of it, I can see that it was. Much
worse than any of us imagined that it even could be.

Everything shifted for a while right after we moved and
then kept shifting after Micah arrived. We all held our
breath, hoping that whatever it was that had been keep-

ing her up at night, making her whisper to herself in the kitchen, making her walk the beach at midnight, was gone. We started eating dinner together again. We went to the movies, went out for ice cream, cleaned the house. We went grocery shopping and clothes shopping, and sewed new curtains for the living room. From the outside we looked like any other family. Two girls, one boy. Parents still in love after more than fifteen years. They kissed on the couch. We wrinkled our noses and said *Eww*. Shana complained about eating vegetables. I grumbled each time I had to clean my room. Micah whined whenever it was bath time. A little bit at a time we started letting out the air that we had been holding in our lungs. A puff at a time, letting the stale breaths of fear spiral away into the sky. If you looked long enough, you could almost see us relaxing into it, four people making plans for a trip to Disney World, thinking about tearing down the wall between the bedroom and the storage space under the stairs to make a third bathroom. You might have seen people getting their teeth cleaned and begging for a new bicycle and trying to find the perfect recipe for ginger cookies. But if you watched closely enough, I think the thing you would have noticed is the one who wasn't doing all those things. The one who was slowly changing into something that none of us would recognize.

I'm standing in the middle of the room that I haven't seen in almost a year. I just stopped coming in here. It wasn't a conscious decision, like one morning I woke up and said, *That's it. No more painting for me.* If I had, I probably wouldn't have left a painting half finished on the easel under the window. I wouldn't have left three brushes standing in a jar on the sill. I for sure wouldn't have left the cap off a ten-dollar tube of burnt sienna. Dust is everywhere. The windows are tinted by it. The paintings stacked three and four deep against the walls are coated in it. Only the couch where my father sleeps most nights seems fairly clean, at least until I sit on it, sending a cloud of dust swirling into the moonlight. She never worked on just one painting, especially toward the end. She always had two or three or more in various stages. Some barely more than a suggestion of what they were going to become. Others seemingly finished except for her signature. The *Ellie* brushed on in red paint. Always red. Sometimes the only red thing on the canvas. A capital *E* followed by a looping line, spiraling like a phone cord across the bottom of the painting.

They are all there in front of me. All four of them just as I remember. One for each of us. Our portraits. The easels are all pointed inward slightly, forming a half circle around the artist who has been missing for more than a year. If I squint my eyes and tilt my head I can imagine her there, standing in front of them, paintbrush dripping blue onto the planked floor. I can see her blond ponytail, twisted around itself and held in place by the tortoiseshell clip she always wore. I can see her stand up on her tiptoes, something she always used to do *to get a new perspective*. I look from one portrait to the next then back again, looking longer at Micah's. His is the one I don't understand. His is the one that scares me.

"Okay, let me get this straight," Raven says. She blows upward so that her bangs float away from her forehead before settling back in place. "Christmas is now green and *pink*? What happened to red?"

Todd keeps stringing the tiny fuchsia lights around the front windows, tacking them in place with bits of gray putty. "Pink is the new red," he says, stepping down off the stool and walking over to where we are standing, unpacking the boxes from the Starbucks corporate offices.

Already we are surrounded by shiny silver garlands, dozens of green Christmas cups, and a huge poster of the Mintaccino. Raven yelled dibs as soon as she saw it, making Todd promise that she could take it home when the holidays were over.

"Micah, try to put ornaments all the way around the tree. Not just in that one spot." Todd walks over to Micah and whispers something that makes Micah crack up. Todd starts moving some of the silver balls to higher branches, humming along to the terrible Christmas music Raven insists we play. So far we have listened to "Grandma Got Run

Chloe

Over by a Reindeer," "I Saw Mommy Kissing Santa Claus," and the one that Micah keeps begging to hear again, "Jingle Bells." Not the normal version with words. This one is all dogs barking. I can hear Micah and Todd *ruffing* and *yapping* in time with the song.

"He's good," Raven says, taking one end of the silver garland from me and tacking it along the front of the counter. She laughs at the look on my face. "Not at singing," she says, shaking her head. "I mean, I do have ears." Todd and Micah howl loudly along with the ending bars. Raven slowly makes her way toward me, tacking the garland to the shelf in even intervals. "I meant with kids." I nod, watching as Todd and Micah start having a sword fight with giant plastic candy canes. I'm smiling at them, but I can't help feeling sad, too. Someone not even related to him, someone he barely knows, can make Micah laugh, while his own family seems to barely be able to keep him from crying. Before the song can start up again, we hear a beeping sound from the other side of the counter.

"Raven, your phone," Todd says, but she's already around the counter and is digging in her bag. She flips her phone open and frowns at it before pushing a button and holding it up to her ear. The barking starts again, making Raven push through the door to the storage room with her other hand pressed over her free ear. All three of us are watching as the door thumps behind her, swinging back and forth in the jam before becoming still.

"I have to go," she says, pushing back through the door, her phone still in her hand, her scarf already twisted around her neck. She freezes when she sees me. "Oh Chloe . . . I . . ."

"I'll get them home," Todd says, stepping toward her, his candy cane still clutched in his hand. "Is everything okay?" Raven looks at him for a moment. She opens her mouth, as if she's about to say something, then closes it and nods.

"Everything's fine. I just need to get home," she says, pushing her arms through the sleeves of her coat. "I'll see you tomorrow," she says. She looks at me for a moment, same open mouth, then just a nod.

"'Night, Raven," Todd says, pushing the door open for her. He follows her out and watches as she walks down the block to her car. He keeps standing there, rubbing his hands up and down his arms until she gets her car started and pulls away from the curb. He lifts his hand as she rolls past and keeps watching until her car is through the intersection and just another pair of taillights going up the hill toward the highway.

"Well, that was random," Todd says, pushing back through the door. He's trying to play it off, but he seems worried. He sighs and rubs his hands together, but then looks at Micah. "Okay then. Where were we?" He bends to pick up the candy cane where he dropped it before going outside. He feigns a stab in Micah's direction, and soon they are at it again, their movements accompanied by a chorus of dogs. "Wait, this isn't right." Todd walks to the back door and disappears into the storeroom. The music stops, and I look over at Micah who is standing there, cheeks flushed and smiling. I just shrug at him and smile back. Suddenly the room is filled with the sounds of cats, meowing and yowling and mewing. After a few notes I can start to decipher a tune. "Much better," Todd says. We keep hanging and tying and fluffing and tinseling until late.

It isn't until I am lying in bed, a box of leftover Christmas decorations sitting in the corner of my room, that I wonder why Todd thought the sound of cats meowing their way through "Rudolph the Red-Nosed Reindeer" was a better choice for fighting with oversize plastic confections than "Jingle Bells." I smile into my pillow as I remember Micah's face when Todd told him he could take the leftover cookies home with him. *To share*, Todd said, wrapping them in plastic wrap and handing them to him. Only my worry about Raven keeps me awake tonight. Finally I fall asleep by clinging to the half smile she gave me before she walked out into the snow.

The reds almost match. Micah's is only the slightest bit darker than the rest of ours. His is almost a cranberry, while ours are definitely more of a claret. Ever since I went into the studio I find myself thinking about color the way I used to. In specific, not general. My mother always told me I had an eye for it, asking for my advice when she had a particularly demanding client. *Do you think that is more sea blue or aquamarine?* she would ask. *Cerulean,* I would say, making the corners of her eyes crinkle as she smiled at me.

I hang Micah's stocking next to my father's, making him share the right side of the hearth. I hang Shana's next, then my mother's, then mine. My mother's is longer than ours—a point we would always argue. *More room for presents,* she would tease. Although on Christmas morning we always found our stockings stuffed with hollow chocolate Santas and colored pencils and pages of stickers, while hers was empty except for a tiny box pushed into the toe. That box was always opened last. Shana and I would press into her, each trying to see inside the box first. She would lift it out and hold it over our faces, letting it dangle and catch the lights of the tree. I remember the last one, the one she didn't get to open. By Christmas morning she was in the hospital. It was Shana who finally had the courage to look inside the box. There, surrounded by tissue, was a tiny baby carriage, this one with an *M* on it. Shana linked it to my bracelet, right between two other charms. The stack of blocks with a *C* on it and the tiny silver shoe with a curly *S* on the side.

Now I finger the links of my bracelet for a moment before plunging my hand back into the cardboard box marked CHRISTMAS in my mother's neat block letters. I lay the angel tree topper on the couch and reach inside again to pull out a tablecloth embroidered with red and green holly.

"Chlo-ee?" Micah is holding a needle in one hand and a short string of popcorn in the other.

"That looks good," I say, walking over to where he is sitting. Bits of popcorn cover his lap and dangle from the cables of his sweater. I take the needle and thread from him, pressing the end through the eye again.

"This is fun," Micah says. His tongue works its way past the corner of his mouth as he concentrates on the next puff, pushing the needle through the center and then pulling it through the other side. He holds up the chain again, showing me his progress.

"You're doing great." He smiles at me and keeps working. Tongue, push, pull, lift, and look. I hear the sound of boots in the hallway. I stand still, holding my breath, but then I hear the key and the door opening. No visit yet, but soon.

"Hey, what are you guys . . ." Shana stops as soon as she rounds the corner into the living room.

"Christmas," Micah says, leaning forward and holding up his popcorn strand. He frowns when she doesn't even glance at his work. Shana looks silently around the room. She smiles when she sees the plastic nativity set, the one we could play with. The one with the slightly gnawed-on Baby Jesus who was rescued with only seconds to spare from an overly playful tabby cat. She smiles bigger when she sees that I have hung all of our old mittens from the curtain rods, looping their strings over the top so that they could dangle down. I keep watching her, finding something I've been missing for a long time in her face. She looks at me, then beyond me to the fireplace.

"Chloe, no," she says, walking past me. She lifts our mother's stocking from its hook and holds it out in front of her. She stands, staring at the gold cord that is twisted and looped to spell *Ellie*. "You can't," Shana says, folding the top of the stocking over until it meets its toe, then folding it again and again until it's just a lump of red in her hand.

"Give it back," I say, putting my hand out. Shana just looks at me and then down at the folded cloth in her hand.

"No," she says.

"Shana, I mean it." I'm aware that Micah has stopped threading his popcorn and is watching us. I reach out and grab the bit of fabric that is sticking out of her fist and pull. We stand like that, each pulling at an end of the stocking. I imagine that I will hear ripping and in a moment we will each be standing here, holding half of a stocking, but then suddenly Shana lets go and I have to step back to keep my balance.

"She's not coming for Christmas," Shana says, her eyes still fixed on the now limp stocking hanging from my hand. "Not this year. Not ever."

"You don't know that," I say, pulling at the edges of the fabric, trying to make it the shape it once was.

"Yes, I do." Shana is looking right at me. We stand like that for a moment before Micah's voice makes us both look over.

"It's good?" he says, holding up his chain, only slightly longer than before.

"It's good," Shana says. She walks over to where he is sitting and bends down over his chain to get a closer look. I'm hanging the stocking back on its hook when I notice the rip. It's not a big one, but it's there. Right on the seam. Right below her name.

CHAPTER FOURTEEN

Shana

IT STARTS OUT as one of my favorite days in a long time. Maybe since *everything happened,* as the social workers always say. I think about that phrase sometimes, like what if everything *had* happened? We'd all just be standing around looking at each other, forever. Anyway, the whole time with Jason, walking out to his car, I keep stealing sideways glances at him. And he's doing the same thing, checking me out. Hard not to do, I guess. I mean, it's like that movie where those guys get the face transplants. Suddenly instead of this bleak and sinister-looking dude in black lipstick and lace-up boots and trench coat, I get some cute guy with a dimple in his chin and hair that curls along his neck, who's wearing under his jacket a T-shirt that says REPUBLICAN SHAMPOO: LIE, STEAL, REPEAT.

I stop and look at him while he scans the parking lot.

"Lose something?" I ask.

He stands on his toes, like that's going to help. He has his hand up, shielding his eyes, and he half-frowns. "My car. Happens about once a week."

"You're kidding."

"Okay, twice a week." He tugs me by the sleeve of my coat and we start walking about three rows over. He looks at me, those Oreo eyes. "This is vaguely embarrassing."

"Well, what does it look like?"

"It's a car. You know, four doors, tires."

"Okay, smart-ass. I got here by way of the bus stop, and I still know where *that* is. I'll leave your sorry butt right here."

"No," he says. "Please." He means the please. You can always tell when someone means the please. "Oh, wait," he says. "Something about a fourteen, I remember that."

"Like row fourteen?" I open the buttons on my coat, suddenly warm.

"Maybe," he says, and starts walking again. "I guess that makes sense."

I bump him with my shoulder. "Man, it's like watching a famous psychic help the police locate a body."

He looks down at me again. So tall. Does wearing black trench coats make you seem shorter? They should publish like *Goth's Weekly*, with fashion tips. "Okay, I know where it is," he says.

"Where?"

"Right behind you." I turn and see a beat-up blue Honda

with a bumper sticker that says WHAT IF THE HOKEYPOKEY IS WHAT IT'S ALL ABOUT? plus one of those Jesus fish on the trunk lid. I tuck away the bumper sticker inside my head, so I can tell Vernon later.

"Nice car," I say, "though I didn't figure you for a Jesus fish."

He shrugs. "Thanks. It's my mother's."

"The car, or the fish?"

"Both." He unlocks the doors, then moves around to the passenger side to open my car door, like we are going on a date in 1955 or something. Then I wonder where we *are* going.

"The Laundromat," he says when I ask him, then points with his thumb at the backseat, where the passengers are two lumpy bags of laundry. "My mom broke her foot. Dog walking accident. Don't ask." He smiles at me. "Anyway, I've been trying to help out a lot more, since it's hard for her to get around. It's almost a desperate situation at this point. I'm down to my very last shirt, pretty much."

I look again at his shirt while he turns the key and clicks his seat belt and adjusts his rearview, like I'm some kind of driver's ed instructor. He turns down the stereo, which is playing something really old, one of those Motown groups where the backup singers wave their arms in unison.

"The music is your mother's, too?" I say, watching the side of his face as he backs out of the space and moves toward the exit. He has the tiniest, faintest lines around his eyes, like his face is already planning how it's going to age. And it looks like a good plan.

"No, that's mine. Harold Melvin and the Blue Notes." He shrugs, blushing, like his choice of music is way more embarrassing than his paper hat was. And I think I know why. I mean, look at me—Goth girl, carrying a bag from Banana Republic.

"Cool," I say, though I never heard of Harold whoever. "And as for your very last shirt," I say, "I like your politics, but that kinda makes no sense."

He drives into an old part of Portland, where the tourists aren't. All along the streets are pawnshops and convenience stores and places with BEER signs in the windows. He pulls into a place called the Sunshine Center Laundromat and turns off the car. Then he looks down at his shirt, tucking in his chin to read it upside down.

"It's like if the Republicans gave a shampoo, they would lie and—"

"Okay, Jason? I understand the *words*. It's just a weird way to insult someone. A shampoo analogy."

He nods. "Speaking of weird," he says, "how come you're so normal?"

Yeah, that's me, Miss Normal. My mother did stuff you hear about on the nightly news, and now she's locked away in a loony bin. My sister collects broken glass. We've adopted a kid who doesn't speak and lives off sugar. Oh, yeah, and I live in a funeral home. And that's just to start. How could I say any of that to him? I was probably way less scary at *night*, all Goth'd out in ripped hose and chains.

"Well, what about you?" I say. "Lemonade boy. Still want to pierce your penis?"

He shrugs, then blushes. "Come on," he says. "Help me out."

We get his laundry going in two different machines, but none of his Goth stuff is to be found. Just polo shirts and jeans and boxer shorts and fleece jackets and a bunch of mom jeans and sweatshirts. When we have it loaded up and running, Jason brings over two of the plastic chairs from the front window and sets them down in front of the machines, and we watch the clothes spin around and around, like we're watching the best TV show we've ever seen.

And then he starts talking, about everything, talking like he had been saving it up for years, just waiting for someone to listen. All about how he learned to read cereal boxes before he could read books, and how he still likes to hunt down obscure cereal brands like Quisp and Frankenberry and King Vitamin (he apparently has a cereal thing). He tells me that there are only two kinds of music, good and bad, and that he'll listen to anything if it's good. He tells me serious stuff, too, like how his dad died when Jason was eleven, while playing a company softball game. A line drive hit him in the chest and stopped his heart, and Jason was right there to see it happen. His mother found Jesus right after, but a kind of New Age version of it, like she thought that church was outmoded and had been replaced by group therapy. She kept freaking out, he said, because he hadn't rebelled, hadn't ever really screwed up or gotten in real trouble—she was sure that meant there was a problem with his development.

"So the fact that you weren't getting in any trouble whatsoever worried her?" I ask him. The machines stop and we start piling his laundry into one of those rolling carts.

"Exactly. She would show me on the news, like the kids that get caught trying to kill half the school, people always say, 'He seemed like such a nice, quiet boy.' She thought that would be me."

"And thus did mild-mannered Jason become Goth kid, roaming the dark streets of Portland." I push the cart to one of the big empty dryers.

"Yes, to make her happy. Then I met you, met some other cool people." He shrugs. "The costume was just the price of admission." He drops quarters into the machine and starts it up, then looks at me, and for the first time in a long time, someone *is* seeing me. The real me, without the white makeup, without the averted eyes, without the anger, without the attitude. Just the me I haven't been since . . . I can't remember. I feel myself blushing, feel his brown eyes on me. It's hard to explain, even to myself. I just feel like a *girl*, and the simplicity of that seems to go right through me. For a moment I am just one thing instead of a thousand, and that one thing is good. A moment like that is like music . . . it floats through the air, moves through and inside you, and you don't need to bother explaining it. I love that.

You can't trust a good day, because it's like it's just setting you up, lifting you up a little so that the bad stuff can get a good shot at you. I keep reminding myself that Chloe doesn't know. She doesn't know what Mom did. So she hangs up Mom's stocking and keeps putting up the pictures with Mom in them, all along the hallway, and she's always talking about stuff we are going to do after Mom comes home. But like I told Chloe, she isn't coming home. I mean, yeah, they are giving her new drugs every day, and she is in therapy and doing all this other crap, and sometime they might release her, even for just a day, maybe. Dad is all over that idea, and so is Chloe, and Micah really doesn't know the damn difference. All of us are stuck inside some Christmas card picture, the happy family reunited to carve the turkey and sing the carols, and if the picture is blurry enough you won't notice the sad eyes, the knotted fists, the fingernails dug into forearms. So, yeah, she might be able to come home, but she can't. She can't come home even if she can. Or maybe she can, and they can all have Christmas without me. And Micah—he'd have to be out of here, too, before something else bad happens. I think about all of this while I'm lying in bed looking up at the ceiling. If I were a normal girl I would be thinking about my Laundromat date, about the perfect little smirky smile Jason has, or the way he blushed when I made him refold his boxers. But I can't. It's like happiness lies just on the other side of some stone wall, and you start climbing the wall, but a team of stone masons is working furiously, adding layers and layers of stone, so the top of that wall is always just past your fingertips.

And so in my second random act of destruction in less than a week, I get up in the middle of the night, take down Mom's stocking where Chloe has put it back on the fireplace. The felt tears easily enough, but I use a knife anyway, standing over the toilet and dropping those little red triangles down into the bowl. When it's all cut up, I push the handle and watch it swirl away forever.

Lately, like in the last week or so, Chloe has started borrowing my stuff—my cashmere sweater, and my short plaid skirt, and my Red Sox babydoll shirt, and my good pair of Docs.

"So what's the deal?" I say, when she comes in to ask for something else.

She looks at me only briefly. It's weird, in the two days since the thing over the stocking, and after I shrugged and lied when she asked me what happened to it, she is more pissed at me than she ever has been, but she still comes in to ask for the clothes. It's almost funny, the sound that comes out of her mouth, trying to be mad and ask for a favor at the same time. Like someone is punishing her by making her ask for sweaters. I could almost laugh, if laughing seemed like an option these days.

"There's no deal," she says. When she looks at me I notice she is wearing makeup. Not Goth, I mean—cheerleader. "I'm going to Starbucks, and I want to look nice."

"You want to look old, you mean," I tell her. "For your new friends."

She shrugs. "So?"

"So, what are you, the mascot? The littlest barista?"

Her face reddens like it's been slapped, and for half a second I try to wish the words back. "Well, let's see," she says. "My friends talk and laugh and make coffee and dress nicely. Yours mope around and dress like vampire clowns and get the crap beaten—"

"Don't—"

"—by drunk rednecks."

I shake my head. "Don't ever talk about that, ever."

She nods, folding and refolding the sweater she has picked up from the crate of them I keep by the door. "That's your solution to everything, isn't it? Don't talk about Mom, don't talk about Dad's problems. You know, sometimes people feel better after they talk about things."

"How Starbucks of you," I say. "You should move to the *other* Portland, where everyone talks about their feelings."

Her eyes tear up. "You are so mean," she whispers, and

for half a second I want to run to her and pull her by the hand and out the door, take her all the way back to Brunswick, all the way back to the beach, back to ten years old again. But I can't, and so instead I watch her leave, first my doorway and then, ten minutes later, through the front door. Out my window I can see her moving down the walk, and my stomach freezes up because I think how she is moving off without me, wearing her sweaters and skirts, full of color while I slowly fade to black and white. "Don't go," I whisper, and my breath steams the windowpane, revealing a faint fingertip *Hi world!* written in backward letters by Chloe, probably last winter, and she is just a blur of yellow and green through the fog of the glass, gone by the time it clears.

Just then there is a knock at my door, and when I turn around, it's Vernon. This is the first time I can remember him venturing upstairs, and he looks like some scared puppy just brought home from the pet store. Well, if puppies wore suspenders and pocket handkerchiefs and T-shirts advertising the Grand Slam breakfast at Denny's. Just for the record, a plate of eggs doesn't look all that appetizing screenprinted on a shirt.

"I'm sorry to startle you," he says, his voice scratchy.

"You didn't," I tell him.

"Oh. Well, maybe I should try again." He smiles, then rubs the back of his neck, blushing a little. "Listen, when you have a minute, come downstairs for a bit, will you?"

"I will take it under advisement," I say. "What's up? Some emergency dusting?"

"Not just now," he says. "But we really need to talk about your dad." He looks at me evenly then, and I see he means it. My stomach knots up for about the tenth time today.

"Give me a few," I say, and he nods and leaves. I turn back and just stand for a bit, still looking out the window, thinking that if I look long enough, Chloe will reappear around the corner. I breathe on the window again to fog it up, look again at the faint words printed there, reading them backward. Then, just before they fade, I use my fist to slowly wipe them away.

CHAPTER FIFTEEN

Chloe

I CAN ACTUALLY hear her voice in my head when I wake up. *My name is Shana. It rhymes with banana. Your name is Chloe. It rhymes with nothing.* I tried for years to find something that rhymes with *Chloe. Snowy. Blowy.* Shana would tell me, *It has to be a thing.* I mean, *Shana* only rhymes with *banana* if you say *banana* like you're from England, but still it's something.

"Chlo-ee!" Micah's voice rings through the apartment. He sounds panicked, but since he's done the same thing every morning for the last nine mornings, I don't worry too much. I push my arms into my sweatshirt and pull it over my head as I make my way down the hall to the kitchen. I had hoped that today, Saturday, I'd be able to sleep in, but with the Christmas countdown well under way, Micah isn't about to be thrown off his advent calendar. "Can I?" Micah asks as I round the corner and step into the kitchen. He stands with his fingers poised over one of the remaining boxes hanging from the picture on the wall.

"Of course," I say. I shake the kettle to make sure there's water in it before turning on the burner. I reach into the cabinet over the coffeemaker and take down one of the blue mugs with seagulls flying around the rim and drop a teabag into it. "So, what did you get today?" Micah holds up a small figure, dressed in mittens and a scarf. "Nice." I watch him add it to the scene that is slowly taking shape on the table. Each day it's another figure that's supposed to add up to the scene on the cover of the calendar box. Then I fill my mug from the kettle before shutting off the burner. Then I walk to the refrigerator, take the carton of cream out and tip some of it into my mug. Micah keeps arranging the figures around the Christmas tree. "Who's that?" I ask, pointing at the small boy with the green cap.

"Me," he says, smiling up at me. It's a game we've been playing since he started his calendar. So far he has himself, Dad, me, and Vernon. "This one's Shana," he says, holding up his latest figure, the one dressed in blue leggings with yellow hair spilling out from under a matching blue hat. "From before," he says, nodding at me. I nod back, but have to blink hard to keep my eyes from watering. *From before.*

"You hungry?" I ask. I take a swallow of my tea, feeling it burn against my tongue. Micah only nods as he tries to snap a plate of cookies to the dad figure's hand. "What do you want? Pancakes? Cereal?"

Chloe

"You pick," he says, turning to smile at me before going back to work.

"Pancakes then," I say, taking the box of mix out of the pantry. I line up the ingredients on the counter. Cinnamon, vanilla, egg, milk. I place the skillet on the stove, adjusting the flame under to slowly heat it.

"Chlo-ee?" Micah says, his back still to me.

"Yes?" I crack the egg on the side of the bowl, watching as it slowly slides into the mound of mix. He doesn't say anything, making me turn toward him. "Micah?" He looks over his shoulder at me. "What do you need?" He holds the Shana figure up in my direction.

"Another," he says.

"Tomorrow."

He shakes his head. "Another," he says again, pointing at the calendar.

"Another what?" I ask, my fingers still sticky with egg.

"Fig-ure," he says, careful with the word. I watch him silently as he turns the Shana figure toward himself, smoothing the yellow plastic hair with his fingertip. His voice is low when he says it, but it seems to fill up the kitchen, the apartment, then my whole world. "Mother," he says. Then again. "Mother."

I double-check the address I wrote on the back of the napkin: 387 Houston Apt C. I can see apartment A and B from the sidewalk, but there's no C. I look at the napkin again, triple-checking. Todd told me he'd drive me as soon as he could get away, but I didn't want to wait. It's been a week since Raven left in a hurry, pushing out into the snow. It's been a week since she's made it in to work.

"I'm not supposed to do this," Todd said, sliding Raven's employee file from the manila folder. He hesitated again.

"Please, Todd," I said, staring down at my shoes. "I'm worried." I held my breath while he looked at me.

"Me, too," he said, laying the sheet on the desk. "When she called I asked if she was sick." I nodded. "She said no, but her voice got all funny." Todd rubbed his palm against the side of his face. "That was three days ago." I bent and scribbled the address on the back of a napkin and folded it into my pocket.

"I don't like the idea of you going over there alone," Todd said.

"I won't," I lied. "I'll have my father take me." The irony is that having my father drive me over would probably be more dangerous than taking the bus. He is so out of it most of the time that I doubt that he could get us there and back in one piece. I briefly thought of asking Shana to come with me, but after the nasty way she talked to me last time I mentioned Raven, I decided that might be dangerous in a different way.

"You lost?" The voice makes me jump and I drop the folded napkin into the snow. "Didn't mean to scare you." A guy with a brown leather coat and a green scarf is standing in front of me on the sidewalk. He shifts one of his grocery bags to his other hand to pick up the napkin. His guitar case swings forward around his shoulder as he reaches down. He hands the napkin back to me and looks right at me and smiles.

"Thanks," I say quietly.

"It's just that we don't get a lot of visitors over this way." He pauses and looks at the short strip mall across the street where it seems you can get a tan, a movie, a tattoo, or a beer. "At least not so many during the day." He smiles at me again. "Wait a minute," he says, squinting at me. "You're not one of those Mormons, are you?" I shake my head. "Well, then. Girl Scout cookies?" Another shake. "Mary Kay? Avon? Amway?" I keep shaking my head, but by this time I'm smiling.

"I'm looking for someone," I say. "Raven Holmes."

"A friend of Raven's, huh?" he looks at me for a long moment. "I can take you to her if you can answer one very important question." I tilt my head at him. "Have you or have you not had the chicken pox?"

"I have."

"Well, then, Friend of Raven, come with me." He shifts his grocery bags back into both hands and starts up the sidewalk, but before he reaches the porch he makes a hard right and heads around the side of the building. "By the way," he calls over his shoulder, "my name is Sean." I don't get a chance to answer before he's already halfway up a set of stairs clinging to the side of the garage. It's loud back here, with the whizzing of half a dozen whirligigs and the ringing of several wind chimes. As if reading my mind Sean stops halfway up the steps and turns toward me. "You should see this place in the spring. There are flowers everywhere." I follow him up the rest of the stairs and stand a couple of steps below the landing while he unlocks the door. "Rave?" He pushes the door open and calls again, this time his voice is softer. I can hear the familiar clanging and boinking of cartoons in one of the rooms to the right and the sound of a kettle whistling to my left.

"Tea?" Raven calls.

"Yes, please," Sean says, placing the bags of groceries on the floor so that he can lift his guitar case off his shoulder. "You?" he asks me. I nod. "Better make it two," he says.

"Two?" Raven asks, coming around the corner. "Are you that cold?" She stops suddenly. "Chloe?" For a second I'm afraid that it was a mistake coming here. Her face is still for a moment, considering something, but then she pushes past the grocery bags and wraps her arms around me. "Wait," she says, pulling back from me. "Have you had—"

"I already asked her," Sean says. I nod anyway.

"Okay then," Raven says, and she looks at me again for a moment. "You've met my *baby* brother," she says, smirking at me. Sean is a good eight inches taller than either of us. "I have someone else for you to meet." She smiles when she says it, but then she bites her lip. Nervous. I follow Raven down the hall, leaving Sean to sort through the grocery bags. The familiar sounds of SpongeBob's laughter gets louder as we round the corner. Snuggled deep under a bright orange blanket is a little girl. "This," Raven says, "is Izzy . . . my daughter." Izzy looks over at me and waves slightly before turning back to the television. "Surprised?" she asks, looking over at me.

"A little," I say.

"A little." Raven tilts her head at me.

"Maybe a little more than a little."

"Mommy, I think I'm done with cartoons." Izzy is so far down in the blankets that all I can see of her is a splash of dark hair and a bit of forehead peppered with pink spots. Raven goes over and untangles the blanket from Izzy's legs.

"You need anything, bug?"

"I'm just sleepy," Izzy says softly, but it seems she's asleep almost before she can finish talking.

We sit around a kitchen table covered with an oilcloth printed like a picnic blanket with ants all over it.

"Izzy's into bugs," Raven says as we sit down. "So—" Raven begins, but then she stops.

"I think this is a first. She's at a loss for words," Sean says from across the kitchen. He catches a piece of toast in mid-air as it pops from the toaster. "So, Chloe," he says, scraping butter across the surface of the bread. He looks at me for a long moment, tilting his head to one side. "Apricot, right?" I smile and nod at him. "Rave?" Sean asks, his head halfway into the refrigerator. "Where do we keep the jam?" Raven rolls her eyes at me.

"I'm sorry I didn't tell you," Raven says. She takes a sip from her tea, letting it sit for a moment inside her mouth before she swallows. Exactly the way Shana drinks hot things. "I'd like to say it just didn't come up, but it's not that exactly."

"This is what you were talking about a few weeks ago. Is this the complicated stuff?"

Raven nods and sips at her tea again. "It's just that I haven't been working there that long. I haven't known any of you that long." She sighs and sips at her tea again. "It's just not the easiest thing to bring up, you know?" I nod. I do know.

"Ah ha," Sean says, lifting the jar of jam over his head. "Now who's the genius?"

"I'm not sure finding a jar of jam in a refrigerator makes you a genius," Raven says, smiling at me.

"Genius-like."

"Now you know why I haven't been at work this week," Raven says. "What with Sean in school all day and then gone most afternoons and evenings giving guitar lessons over at the university . . . and it's not like she can actually go to school. . . ."

"Why didn't you call me?" I ask. "I mean, I couldn't help you out during the day until school is out, but I could have

Chloe

watched Izzy at night while you were at work." Raven takes another sip of tea.

"I told you," Sean says to Raven. He sets the plate with toast on it in front of me. "Raven doesn't like to impose."

"It wouldn't be an imposition," I say, looking from Sean to Raven.

"Raven has some issues with asking people for things."

"Then I won't make her ask," I say to Sean. "I'm just going to tell her to bring Izzy to my house on the way to work tonight. She can just chill out on the couch and watch cartoons or we'll play board games or color." I am already planning the afternoon. "Micah will be so happy to have someone there to play with."

"Sounds good to me," Sean says, picking up one half of my toast and taking a bite. "Rave?" Sean asks around a mouthful of apricot.

"Sounds like you two have it all planned out," she says, smiling. "Guess I better go call Todd and tell him I'll be in tonight."

"Ah yes," Sean says, sitting down in the chair that Raven just vacated. "Todd . . ."

"Not one more word," Raven says, walking from the kitchen into the back of the apartment. She turns and feigns a stern look. "From either of you." We both pantomime locking our lips with a key. Raven just rolls her eyes. This time at both of us. I realize for the first time in almost a week that my cheeks are hurting again from all the smiling.

"Can someone get that?" I yell for the second time, gathering several paintbrushes in one hand. The ringing of the doorbell turns to knocking and I sigh, kicking the stack of paper in front of me and out of the studio before pulling the door shut. I drop the brushes and the tubes of paint onto the kitchen counter as I walk through to the front hallway. Micah is standing there, his fingers working slowly at the nails of his other hand. "Where's Shana?" I ask, but he just shakes his head. He's nervous about Izzy's visit. He's never had anyone come over to play before. I pull the door open to let Raven in, but it isn't Raven at the door, but Sean.

"Hey there, Chloe. I'm sorry about busting in on you like this. Raven was running late, so I dropped her first." All I can see of Izzy is a red-mittened hand clutching at Sean's leg. I step back to let them in. Izzy is holding on so tightly that it makes Sean look like he's losing in a three-legged race. "Man," Sean says, stopping suddenly. "What is that smell?" I start to answer, but the feeling of Micah's hand slipping into mine makes me stop.

"Brownies," Micah says softly.

"Are you joking me?" Sean asks. Micah shakes his head.

"You understand that brownies are not a joking matter,"

Sean continues. Micah nods his head and smiles. "I'll bet that someone else here likes brownies." Sean tries to turn in a circle, but Izzy is too quick for him, keeping him between herself and us. "I can't quite remember who. . . ." He stops turning and tilts his head, as if thinking.

"Me?" The tiny voice comes from behind Sean's back.

"No, no," he says waving his hand in the air. "Don't tell me. I'll remember it."

"Me," the voice says a bit louder.

"Wait, I think it's coming to me."

"It's me," Izzy says, coming out from behind Sean to tug at his arm.

"Oh yes, that's right. It *is* me." Both Micah and Izzy are laughing now. Sean hands Micah a plastic bag. "Izzy wanted you to see these." He bends to help Izzy out of her coat as Micah peers into the sack.

"Cool," he says, reaching his hand into the bag and pulling out a handful of plastic bugs.

"That's a red-headed centipede," Izzy says, touching one of the bugs with her finger. "And that one's a—"

"Hissing cockroach," Micah finishes. I raise my eyebrows at Sean, but he just shrugs. "See my bugs?" Micah asks. Izzy nods.

"Has he had chicken—" Sean starts to ask.

"Last year," I tell him. He nods.

"Micah's bugs are real," I tell Izzy.

"Cool," she says, following Micah down the hall.

"Why spots?" Micah asks, referring to the bumps on her face.

"I have chicken pox," Izzy says as they turn the corner into Micah's bedroom. We can hear them clucking to each other before dissolving into laughter.

"Okay then," Sean says, smiling at me.

"Okay then," I say. I can feel myself blushing a bit as he looks at me.

"You have the number at Starbucks," Sean says. I nod. "Let me give you my cell, too," he says. "Just in case." I write the number on the erase board above the phone in the kitchen.

"Listen, Chloe," Sean says, pulling the door open. I can feel the cold air spiral in from the hallway. "You're a lifesaver." I smile at him, but as soon as the door shuts I feel the smile fading. Saving lives is not something I've been that good at in the past.

"Okay," Dad says. His voice is too loud, and it cracks, as if he's just trying it out for the first time. "I have a surprise." Micah smiles big, still glowing from his first playdate the night before. "Anyone want to guess?" he asks. I look at Shana, sitting sipping her coffee, one mouthful at a time. She briefly cuts her eyes at me before answering.

"You've decided to quit smoking," she says. I can see the light in Dad's eyes dim a bit.

Stop, I mouth at her, but she just shakes her head slightly.

Chloe

"Umm." His voice cracks this time again. "No." Micah starts working his fingers again, something I haven't seen him do since Izzy arrived. "Guess who's coming for Christmas?"

"You mean besides Santa Claus?" Shana asks.

He nods. "Well, not actually on Christmas," he says. "Kind of like early Christmas." He looks like he's about to burst, but he waits for us to guess again.

"The Hanukkah Elf?" Shana asks. I kick at her leg under the table, but all I end up kicking is air.

"Not even close," he says.

"The Kwanzaa . . ." Shana pauses.

"Elf?" I ask her, but she just waves her hand at me.

"Maybe the Solstice Snowflake."

Dad is shaking his head and smiling. "Guess again," he says.

"Dad, who?" I ask.

"Mom," he says. It's as if time slows for one moment, pulling away from us then pushing back at us.

"What did you say?" Shana asks. Her voice is lower. All the playfulness is gone.

"Mom's coming home for Christmas," he says, smiling. "Well, just for one day, but the therapist says that's the first step."

"The first step toward what?" Shana asks. Her hands are shaking.

"The first step toward her coming home for good."

Shana pushes away from the table, knocking her chair backward with a bang. I hear her boots on the wood floor, then the sound of the front door slamming.

"Are you surprised?" Dad asks me, as if nothing just happened.

"Yes," I say, staring down at my fingers, splayed across the tablecloth.

Dad starts listing all the things we need to do to get ready for her visit. "Buy a tree, bake cookies . . ." His voice gets fainter as he walks into the kitchen, but I can still hear him making his list. Only Micah hasn't said anything at all. I look across at him, where he has his fingers splayed across the table, too, only there's one difference: the whole side of his index finger is red with blood from where he tore at it with his nails.

Chloe

CHAPTER SIXTEEN

Shana

I HEAR VERNON before I can see him. He's in Dad's office with the door closed, a low *thump, thump, thump* sounding against the wall. I stand just outside, trying to figure out what the sound might be, aside from some kind of B movie mortuary sound effects, but after six more *thumps* I still can't pin it down. Finally I knock on the door as I slowly push it open.

"Vernon? Is that you?"

"FORE!" he yells, and a final *thump* sounds just on the other side of the door, at head height. I peek around the edge of the door. Darts. Vernon is playing darts.

"You know," I tell him, "I've been wanting more piercings, but I'd prefer something a little more accurate."

"I guess I ought to lock that door more often," he says. "I could put out an eye with those things."

"Spoken like a true mom," I tell him. He smiles, and both of us let the awkward moment pass. "So, what's up?"

He looks around the office. "I got a new dartboard," he says.

"Vernon, you said you wanted to talk to me about Dad."

He frowns and offers me the final two darts. I move beside him, toss, and stick it right in the door. "Well, you have other talents, I'm sure," he says. "And that was two days ago I told you I wanted to talk about your dad."

"I was busy," I tell him. I throw the other dart and it sticks into the calendar hung beside the door, right between the two puppies and their ball of yarn. "And what's the deal with that picture," I say. "Kittens play with yarn balls, not dogs."

"Busy doing what?"

I shrug. I can't tell him, or anyone, that I have been busy in my room, downloading Greyhound bus schedules, or seeing how far an airplane will take me for $125. Little runaway, milk-carton Shana—I know how it will look. The cops will tell Dad to give it a day, because—heh, heh—you know those kids get hungry and come rolling on home by suppertime. But I'm serious. If she's here, I'm leaving. And I know how things work. One visit here that's not a total disaster, and the doctors and all those other idiots will be saying what fine progress she's making, and how therapeutic it is for her to be here. Well, fine, but I'm not on this earth for therapeutic purposes, especially not hers. I can't, not ever, not after what she did. And that Dad would allow it, *welcome* it, is beyond me. I mean, really, I don't get it. So, let her come here. I won't be anywhere around. The only monkey wrench in my plans? I don't have anywhere to go. The closest relative is some third uncle twice removed or something, out in some little town in Michigan, living in a trailer. I don't think so.

Vernon cracks his knuckles. "All right then. The silent treatment. I've had that from women before, you know. Tougher nuts than you. So, we'll talk about your dad, but we should get away from this place. We can't talk here."

"Why not here?" I ask, lowering my voice to a whisper.

Vernon shifts his eyes back and forth, then lowers his own voice. "Because," he says, "it's my lunch hour. I'm hungry."

"Lunch" turns out to be hot dogs and Cokes from the snack bar at the Candlepin bowling alley, which is about two blocks away from where Jason took me for laundry. We step inside, and the smell hits me first, a combination of floor wax and onions and Lysol. We order our hot dogs and sit on the revolving stools.

"I gotta stop going on dates in the bad part of town," I tell him, pulling another paper napkin from the dispenser. "I might get a reputation."

"You should've worn your costume," he says, chewing. "Scare off all the bad guys."

"It's not a 'costume,' Vernon," I tell him, though I remember as I say it that Jason called his Goth stuff the same thing. And that's exactly what it is, I guess—just a disguise.

"What is it then?" he asks.

I twist my mouth, thinking. "A lifestyle."

"Pffft." Vernon shakes his head. "How come everybody but me has a 'lifestyle'? I just have a life."

I shrug. "Because you are one of a kind," I tell him. "Now, fill me in on Dad."

"Shana," he says, "it's not good."

He finishes his third hot dog with everything and tugs my sleeve toward the back of the bowling alley. All around us is this echoey sound of the pins falling down, the balls rolling on the metal rails and clacking into one another. It turns out we are here not for the bowling, but for the claw machine in the back, next to the pool table. Vernon feeds several dollars into the machine and starts working the buttons. On the very first try he wins a stuffed Scooby-Doo.

"That was lucky," I say.

"Ha."

"Vernon . . . Dad?"

He nods, working the lever again. A miss this time. "Already he's had the IRS nosing around, and then the very next day an examiner from the bank, and next week some coat and tie from the Board of Funeral Licensure. They're going to close him down, Shana. He has been screwing up, bad. Excuse my French."

I smile a little as I watch him win again, this time a stuffed Buzz Lightyear. He hands them to me like they are made of gold, then goes right back to playing. In the meantime, my stomach has become a centrifuge, spinning around all that hot dog and Coke. I mean, suppose Dad goes to *jail*? Then what? What happens to us? We'll end up like those people on crappy daytime TV, siblings reunited thirty years after tragic circumstances tore them apart. That's how they always say it. Will that be us? I think about not seeing Chloe, not seeing Micah, and it feels more like I am being torn apart by wild dogs instead of circumstances, and I know right then that I'm not going anywhere. Not by Greyhound, and not on a plane. Something has to happen, something else, but I'm not leaving them.

"So, is it too late to do anything? I mean. . . ."

He shrugs and misses again, frowns. I'm throwing him off his game. "The IRS will chew his butt, for sure. But that's just fines. The board can shut him down, the bank can send him to jail. But, see, sweetie, people don't like to do those things."

"Why?"

"Because it makes work for them. I'm sorry, but that's how the world is." He wins again, the claw dragging a stuffed toy carrot over the chute and dropping it down. "You know, back in the day you worked these things by hand, a little crank and a wheel, not all this electronic stuff."

"And you'd win rocks and celebrate with a communal hunt?"

He glances at me. "Smart-ass. I'm not as old as you think. Go ahead and guess."

"Seventy-three," I say.

"Damn. I guess I am, after all."

"No, you told me already. So, listen, we're okay for now, with Dad?" I feel the centrifuge in my stomach slowing just a little.

"No. We're not. I don't know what's going to happen. But I'll tell you what . . . you and I are taking over. Me and you. We'll do it all, and your dad can sit around on the roof all he wants."

"But he'll know what we're doing. I mean, we can't just sweep him aside like that. It is *his* business."

Vernon plays his last game on the claw machine, a miss. "Sweetie, have you really even talked to him lately?" He shakes his head. "I mean, the lights are on, but nobody's home."

And so I try, talking to him.

He is home every day now, since his big announcement, getting the house ready, as he calls it. He already bought and put up a tree in the TV room, even though it's too early and the tree will likely be dead and brown by Christmas morning. He painted half of the hallway, then quit before he finished and moved on to something else, half panicked energy and half drunken forgetfulness.

"Dad," I finally say to him one morning.

He stops mopping the kitchen floor and looks at me. Micah is on the floor (for some reason, he has never liked chairs very much) eating strawberry Pop-Tarts and stacking up plastic bottle caps he has found in the trash.

Dad smiles at me, his hair sweaty and stuck to his forehead, his face stubbly and dark. He is wearing one of his white dress shirts over his shorts with the flames up the sides. "Yes, sweetheart?" he says.

"Dad, we can't. Don't let her come here." I cut my eyes at Micah, careful of my words.

He nods, but it's like he's nodding at something else, not at what I just said. "Your mom belongs here, Shana. This is her home."

Micah puts his Pop-Tart flat on the floor and sets the bottle caps on top of it, like little people stranded on a raft.

"You're dreaming up clichés," I tell him. "How about, this is her home, and she doesn't belong here. That's really the truth."

"No, no. No. It'll be fun, I promise."

"Fun." I feel my heart starting to whir like some broken machine, stuck on overdrive. Micah leans both hands into the bottle caps he's placed on the Pop-Tart, and finally it makes sense, what he's doing, using the caps like little cookie cutters, making half a dozen little disks of strawberry Pop-Tart.

Dad pushes his hair off his forehead, and it stands straight up from the sweat.

"Shana," he says, "it's Christmas."

I nod, unable to look at him anymore. "God bless us, every one," I say, with as much nastiness as I can conjure up. Dad sighs, still looking at me. I shake my head. "Have you forgotten what. . . ." I wipe my eyes with the back of my thumb. I look at Micah, who is now peeling apart the disks and sticking them to his hand, jam side down. I tip my chin at him and try again. "Look at him," I say to Dad. "Have you forgotten what she did?"

He blinks several times behind his glasses, like maybe he *has* forgotten. "She has a problem, Shana."

I half laugh. "Yeah."

Dad shakes his head. "For godsakes . . ."

Just then Micah peels away the little disks of pastry and eats them, one at a time. When they're gone he looks at his hand, holding it up like it's not his hand at all, and he starts breathing hard, sucking in whole breaths, and it takes me half a second before I see what he's seeing—the whole front and back of his hand smeared red with the strawberry jam.

"Dad—" I jump up from my chair.

". . . she's your *mother.*" He finishes his sentence, his

Shana

voice coming down like a blade on the last word, and by then Micah has his mouth open wide, and the screams start pouring out of him. And they don't stop until I am holding him, holding his hand under a stream of warm water in the kitchen sink, washing him clean while Dad walks out of the room.

"You think they purposely make store brands crappy," Jason says, "or do they just make them cheap and they turn out crappy?"

He has brought me along to help with the grocery shopping he does once a week for his mother. Already he's spent five minutes talking about Treet, wondering if it was made for people who one day *aspired* to Spam. For half a second, I wonder if he might be Vernon's long-lost son. I also wonder if every date we have, if we are in fact dating, will involve some domestic chore. "I'd say they make them cheap," I say. "Crappiness is just a side effect."

He nods, turns the cart down the next aisle. "Interesting. So, the taste is just a function of cheaper, inferior ingredients?"

"No, they buy in bulk, so cost isn't an issue. Cheap is to increase profit. They taste bad because consumers want it that way." I look over at the list he's scrawled on the back of a napkin and toss a can of coffee into the cart.

He looks at me. "They do?"

"People who live cheap enjoy the sacrifice. Why else

would they buy twenty-five-watt lightbulbs? They live in the dark so they can save, what? Four dollars a year? Enduring the taste of Oatie-O's, knowing you could have Cheerios, is the real pleasure of eating them, not that sixteen cents you saved."

He smiles. "Pretty smart."

"You mean, of course, pretty and smart, yes?"

He actually blushes. "Yes. That's what I said."

Since my talk with Dad, since Micah, I have been away from the house as much as I can be. Only a week now until she is home, and I don't know what to do. I mean, I'm just the kid, and the kid doesn't get the final say. So for now, distraction is working, and Jason is distraction.

He decides to leave the groceries and for us to take a walk in Old Port, since the weather is cold enough to keep stuff from spoiling in the car. We move down the sidewalks, our breath visible in the cold as we step around icy patches. We pass the side street where the fight happened, and it's weird—it's like for the first time I really make the connection, that it was *him*, this Jason, with me there that night, his mouth bleeding.

"I try not to think about it," he says, as if reading my thoughts, "but I do."

I nod. "Everything felt different after that. Just . . . I don't know. It's like my life didn't quite fit me right after that night. The sleeves were too short or something."

"Yeah, the whole time I kept thinking, *I'm not the kind*

of person this happens to, I don't get beaten up in alleys. Then, I mean, what kind of person *does* that happen to? After that, Chick-fil-A didn't seem so awful, you know?"

"Yeah, I do know."

"Getting beat up made my mom happy, though." He looks at me when I laugh. "Do you think you'll ever go back?" he asks.

"To that street?" I say. Sometime in the last five minutes Jason has taken my hand to steer me around an ice puddle, and has not let go. "That bar?"

"No. I mean to the clothes, the stuff. Will you go back to Goth again? I don't know. . . ." He squeezes my hand. "It just seems different now. No more costumes."

I want to tell him no, I will never go back, I will always be me. But with everything coming at me, I can't. Even next week, I'm looking ahead to one day when I will want to hide completely, when I will want to be anyone other than me. Jason senses my hesitation, squeezes my hand.

"Why?" he says.

I stop and look at him, and I want to tell him everything. All of it, all the crap I am hiding from. But there's just too much of it. He was hiding out. Why? Because he was a little lonely, a little sad about his father? I'm hiding out because my life is a train wreck involving tanker cars full of chemicals, any one of them about to explode any second now. I just shake my head and say nothing.

We are passing Starbucks before I even realize it, the

big front window with its stuffed chairs, people sitting in them laughing, leaning in to talk, and other people with Christmas shopping bags leaning against their legs, warming their hands on cups of coffee, music and warmth pouring out the front door.

"Hey, there's your sister," Jason says. "Let's go in."

I look toward the back of the store and see her there, sitting with Micah, who is eating a cookie off a napkin and drinking hot chocolate, his mouth ringed by it. And there is some other kid there I don't recognize, some dark-haired girl about Micah's age, and they are making a game of trading bites of cookie. And then Chloe's new friend walks over, the one who works there—Raven, I remember. That's her name. Only she is not in uniform this time. She's just sitting and eating cookies like everyone else. While we watch she finishes making this long straw by joining like five straws together, and Micah has to stand in his chair to drink from it. They are all laughing now, and every time someone opens the door to leave I think I can hear them, or that maybe the music is the sound of their laughing, and I keep thinking that Chloe will look up and see me there, but she doesn't. And then it hits me . . . I don't want her to. She is having so much fun, all of them. They look like best friends, with little kids. Chloe looks happy, and I know if she sees me, it will just mean another fight, another rip in another Christmas stocking, more random destruction. They all look so happy . . . they look like family. And maybe that's it—if your family is broken and ruined, go find another one, or better yet, go make another one.

"Are we going in, or not?" Jason says.

"I think not," I tell him. I look at him and force a smile. "Let's just keep walking, it's too crowded in there."

"That other girl, next to your sister . . . she looks familiar," Jason says. "Who is she?"

I tug his hand to move on down the sidewalk. "Her name is Raven," I say, almost whispering. "Chloe's other sister."

That night I'm downstairs late, helping Vernon. Our first step is just to organize everything, or try to. Try to get all the paperwork and check stubs organized into boxes. Vernon takes a break to coach me in darts, and he orders in a pizza, and he keeps trying to get me to play along, asking me once if I know what he does when he's feeling blue.

"What?" I say, looking up from my work.

"I start breathing again."

I smile, nod. But really I'm thinking. Mom can't be here. She just can't, and no one else but me is going to stop it from happening. But how? I keep thinking that if I could get Dad to call the hospital when he's drunk, they would never let her come here. Those idiots say the words *stable environment* over and over, a mantra. Or maybe I could call and say he's drunk, or I'm drunk or . . . the house is on fire, no visitors today, please.

"Well, here's my question," Vernon says. "If electricity comes from electrons, does morality come from morons?"

I look at him and really do laugh this time. "You know," I say, "I'm beginning to think that's exactly right."

"That's my girl," he says.

It's so simple, really. All it would take was for Dad to call and say *we aren't ready*, and that would be that. Visit canceled. If I call, they will call Dad to double-check. *Poor girl, she is so upset by all of this.* Vernon is still chuckling at his own joke, and I look up at him, just looking until he looks away from his work and looks back.

"Well, I thought it was funny," he says.

"Listen," I say, "you want to help me keep things from getting any worse around here?"

"They can get worse?"

I nod. "Way worse. Trust me."

"I do trust you. And no, young lady, I don't want that."

"Good, then I need you to do something for me," I tell him. "I need you to make a phone call."

Shana

CHAPTER SEVENTEEN

Chloe

THE NOT KNOWING is always worse than the knowing. Okay, so it isn't some big epiphany or anything, but it's the best reason I can come up with for why I'm feeling so freaked out about Mom visiting. I mean, it's been months since I've seen her. I had to really think about how many, ticking them off in my head by events instead of increments of time. Easter, Mother's Day, summer break, Fourth of July, back to school . . . In between are all the things that just held us together for a while. Groceries, homework, dentist appointments . . . It was as if things were getting slowly better each day just a little bit, bumping along, rocking us slowly with their rhythm like a long car ride with no destination. With Micah and then Raven and then Sean and Izzy and coffee and Christmas, it seemed like I could at least distract myself from the fact that my father was slowly fading away and that Shana was even more of a ghost than when she dressed like one. I could almost feel myself warming up in little ways, even on the inside, which had felt cold for so long.

But that was before Dad's surprise.

I know Shana thinks I'm too young, even though there's just the one year between us, but I get how big all of this is. I get that this visit could mean everything or nothing. I mean, Dad looks like he's about to have a nervous breakdown, and Shana is here even less than before. Micah is just too little, so that leaves me. It's going to be up to me to make it happen, and I'm determined not to let it get screwed up like so many other things have been. Maybe if I hold on to everything tightly enough, it won't fall apart.

So, here I am, in Sean's car, getting a ride to the art store, the good one on the other side of town. The one I always used to go to with Mom, where I know they will still have her favorite stuff. I wouldn't have called Sean in a million years if it weren't for *The Visit*. And I keep thinking of it that way. Capital *T.* Capital *V,* like some bad horror movie that they advertise on MTV during the commercial breaks between bad reality shows.

"Now you," Sean says, cutting his eyes at me before looking back at the road in front of us.

"Leo?" I ask.

"Nope."

"Sagittarius?"

"Not even close," he says, smiling. I watch the side of his

face for a moment before looking back into my lap, where my mittened hands keep pushing at each other.

"I just thought with the music. . . ."

"Nah," he says, making the sweeping curve onto the highway. "I'm not that kind of musician." He rights the wheel and puts one of his hands back on his leg.

"What kind?" I ask.

"The artist kind," he says, looking over at me again. "I have to think my way into it, you know?" I nod. "How about you?" he asks, taking the ramp for South Portland. "Your painting . . . do you have to think it through, or are you the real deal?"

"The real deal, I guess . . ." I say softly, my mittens pushing even harder into each other like they're fighting for space.

"I thought so," he says, slowing to turn into the Paint Box parking lot. "You seem like the sensitive artist type to me." He pulls into the space between the van with the LIVING THE DREAM sticker and the Honda with the broken taillight. I'm out of the car before he can even turn the engine off. I push the door shut, hearing it pop against the frame. I stare at the paintings in the window, trying to think of anything else at all except what I am thinking. *Just like her,* I think, pushing one of my mittens into my eyes, trying to push the tears back inside. *The artist type, the sensitive type, the crazy type.*

+ + +

"So," I say, placing another tube of paint in my basket. We've been in the store for more than twenty minutes, but we've only gotten as far as the paint. We've been doing more talking than shopping.

"So," Sean says, twirling a paintbrush around his fingers, making it freefall around his thumb before pulling it back in.

"You don't really believe in all that astrology junk, do you?"

"Junk?" Sean says, stepping back from me and placing his free hand against his chest. I smile at him. "You mock the astral ways?"

"Astral ways . . ."

"There are higher forces than we can possibly understand. . . ." He starts laughing before he can finish. "Nah," he says, flipping the paintbrush again. "I just like to find out as much as I can about people, you know?"

"Like their signs?" I ask, smirking at him.

"It's sometimes easier than the big stuff." He turns and replaces the paintbrush he's been twirling into the wooden box.

"Yeah," I say, staring down at the toes of my hiking boots peeking out from below my cords. I keep thinking about that as we make our way to the back of the store where the paper is kept.

"The thing is," Sean says, taking the basket from me so I can flip through the stacks, trying to find the right cold press paper, "sometimes it feels like you're just going to burst from all the big stuff, like there's no room left for anything else." I look over at him, but he's staring down at his hand, clutching the basket. I slide half a dozen sheets from the rack and tuck them under my arm to keep them from dragging on the floor as we make our way back to the front of the store to check out.

Sean slides the paper into the backseat and rests the bag on the floor behind me. "You ready?" he asks, looking at me briefly before turning to look out the back. I lean my head against the headrest and close my eyes, feeling the car pull back then start forward, bumping twice before turning into the street. "I always get disoriented down here," Sean says. I open my eyes as I feel him slowing down. "That way?" he says to me. "Right?" I nod, before closing my eyes again, but not before I see the big yellow sign at the corner. I breathe slowly, willing the dizzy feeling to stop. *It's true*, I think, breathing again. *It is the not knowing.* I can still see it with my eyes closed, hovering just behind my eyelids. Black letters floating on a sea of yellow. BLIND INTERSECTION AHEAD.

"I called the hospital," Dad says, tipping a stream of cream into his coffee. He's already added it twice, but with the way his hands are shaking, I doubt he's even going to drink it. "Just to double-check the medication. They said the visit's been canceled. They said I called." He frowns into the coffee, and the worst part is I can see that he isn't sure if he actually did cancel it or not. I look over at Shana, but she's looking past me out the window. I keep looking at her, but she just lets her eyes travel over my face and then past it, never meeting my gaze.

"So, the visit's off?" Shana asks. Dad nods, but his eyes don't focus, like he's only half heard her. I see Shana smile slightly, just in her eyes, but it's there. I stare at the side of her face, and she looks over at me, the tiny smile still dancing. I feel the anger inside of me. *She did something.* She raises her eyebrow at me before pushing away from the table and carrying her cereal bowl to the sink. I hear the water splash into the bowl then out.

"Can't you just reschedule?" I ask.

"They started talking about unstable environments and unfocused goals," he says, still staring into his coffee. "So, I told them we'd come there." His gaze is just focused on something far away. He dribbles another stream of cream into his coffee. Shana turns away from the sink, her cereal bowl still clutched in her hand. I'm thinking maybe this is even better, that we can see her there, just to start, that all of us won't be so nervous.

"You told them who'd come there?" Shana asks. Her voice is low, hard.

"All of us," Dad says, smiling down at his mug. He lifts it to his lips. He takes a sip and grimaces as the liquid fills his mouth.

"Not Micah," Shana says.

Chloe

"Of course Micah," Dad says, placing his mug back on the table. "He's part of the family, isn't he?"

"Not Micah," Shana says again, but it isn't clear whether Dad hears her. He dribbles more cream into his mug. We hear a thud then from Micah's room, probably his books falling off the shelf again, or his pirate ship. About two seconds later, he starts to cry.

"You okay, Micah?" I say, pushing to standing. "Dad, Micah," I say, but when I look back over my shoulder before heading down the hall, he's still sitting there, stirring his coffee, watching as it swirls around and around.

At first, they let her make phone calls. Always on Sunday. Always in the evening. Dad knew ahead of time, but sometimes he'd forget to tell us. One time I picked up the phone, figuring it was someone from school or one of Shana's weird Goth friends, but it wasn't any of those. It was her. They call making phone calls a *life skill*. Dad said that Mom was working on the class one skills, things like personal hygiene and doing laundry and managing small sums of money and phone calls. We even got a box with a lot of brochures and a videotape that we were supposed to watch. *Living with Paranoid Schizophrenia.* I was the only one who watched it. They kept referring to "interfacing with the patient," "managing symptoms," and "coping with episodes." A lot of "ing" verbs that mostly meant things were always going to be different.

That night I could hear the caseworker through the phone. Could hear her prompting my mother to ask me things. We made it through hello and how are you and how is the weather and then there was silence. "Baby," my mother said finally, her words thick and slow, "I miss you." I could hear the caseworker telling her that it was time to hang up, but not before Mom said one more thing. This time softer. "When can I come home?" I didn't know what to tell her.

They say in the darkest parts of insanity there is lucidity, and I guess that's right, but that sounds like something Shana might say. I say in the midst of craziness something normal occasionally happens. I keep having to blow the crepe paper off my face as Micah and Izzy try to attach my antennae. We're having a Bug Ball. Dancing is optional, but costumes are required. Already I've made butterfly wings out of mesh fabric and bent coat hangers and tarantula legs out of my father's black socks stuffed with cotton batting.

"Chlo-ee," Micah says as I blow upward again to keep the pink streamers from sticking to my lips. "Stop." He smoothes the paper back over my face while he twists the ends over and under my headband. The oven timer saves me for a moment and I push to standing. After a brief meeting, we decided that the proper bug lunch would be mini peanut butter and jelly sandwiches, grapes, milk and, of course, bug cookies. I peek into the oven, seeing the chains of rainbow-colored balls that are meant to be caterpillars

Chloe

slowly spread as they bake. Setting the timer for three more minutes, I plunge my hands into the soaking mixing bowl to wash off the last of the batter. I add another squirt of soap into the sink and dump in the two rubber spatulas, licked nearly clean by two now rainbow-colored tongues. Just as I am drying my hands the doorbell rings. I walk back through the living room, stepping over a mound of play pillows, several islands of craft supplies, and a blanket already set for the buggy lunch.

"Chloe," Izzy calls as I reach the door. "Do you have any glitter?"

"Just a minute," I say, peering through the peephole. I've read that your heart can accelerate faster than any performance car when you're frightened. That the saying "my heart jumped into my throat" isn't completely in your mind. When your heart beats that hard and that fast, the extra force of the blood roaring through your arteries can actually make it feel like something jumps inside of you. I don't even bother to look behind me. I know what the place looks like, and no amount of stalling is going to give me time to get it all cleaned up. I flip the latch and turn the knob, pulling the door toward me.

"Chloe, right?" The woman says, tucking a file under her arm. I just nod and step back. I was right. No amount of studying or planning was going to get us ready for this visit. "Is this an okay time?" she asks, but I can tell it's just the thing she says. Ms. Ballentine smiles briefly, lifting a hand to her head as she looks at me. I instinctively touch my head, feeling the streamers that are still tied to my headband. "Mind if I have a look around?" she asks, stepping past me and toward the living room. A trail, like some reverse treasure map, begins with a lone chartreuse crayon.

"Just let me—" I start, but the timer in the kitchen begins beeping again.

"You better get that, dear," Ms. Ballentine says. "Something smells delicious." I pull the cookie sheet out of the oven and place it on top of the stove, twisting the oven dial to off. I hear Ms. Ballentine's voice in the other room, and then Micah's and Izzy's laughter. I lean my forehead against the coolness of the refrigerator and will my heart to slow down. I concentrate on the sounds of the oven popping as it cools, the low swish of the dishwasher as it switches from wash to rinse, and the steady rhythm of the kitchen clock as Elvis's hips click off the seconds. I slide several cookies onto a plate; grab the jug of milk from the refrigerator and a tower of plastic cups from the cabinet. The sound of laughter again, this one punctuated by a low thud, sends me into the living room. I nearly drop the plate of cookies when I round the corner. There in the middle of the picnic blanket is Ms. Ballentine, her head covered in a mound of streamers similar to mine, save for the fact that they are blue and not pink. She blows upward, making the streamers flutter for a second before they rest against her cheeks again.

Chloe

"Hold still," Izzy says, adding another length of ribbon to one side. I walk over to the coffee table and find a bit of clear space to unload my hands. I sit on the edge of the couch cushion, watching as Micah and Izzy turn Ms. Ballentine into a living Maypole, adding fabric and ribbon and crepe paper one piece at a time, standing back occasionally to survey their work.

"How are you?" Ms. Ballentine asks me before taking a bite of one of the cookies. Izzy and Micah are now flopped on the blanket, their hands sticky with peanut butter and their mouths ringed with milk. I shrug, unsure of the right answer, and also of the truthful one.

"Okay," I finally say, and I think that's about as close as I will be able to get.

"Where's everyone else?"

"Dad's downstairs," I say, praying she won't go check. "And Shana's . . . out Christmas shopping." I'm not sure where Shana is, and I'm not sure what she's doing, so that seems as likely as anything else. I keep working at my thumb, peeling off bits of my cuticle with my fingernail.

"Chlo-ee?" Micah says. I look up and see him shaking his head as he watches my fingers. We made a pact after Shana and I found him in the bathroom, one side of his thumbnail exposed all the way down to the base. *I won't rip at my hands if you don't*, I told him. I smile briefly at him, and he goes back to breaking segments from his caterpillar cookie and trying to toss them up and catch them in his mouth.

Ms. Ballentine asks a bunch of questions about what he's eating, how he's sleeping. When she asks how he's doing, I look at him for a second, wondering how any of us are doing right now. He smiles, his mouth covered in crumbs.

"Better," I say.

"Well, Chloe," Ms. Ballentine says, pulling her file folder onto her lap. I can feel the beating again. Zero to sixty in 2.1 seconds. "Things look good." I tilt my head at her. "I mean," she continues, marking something on the top sheet before looking up at me, "things look normal." She dusts the bits of glitter and cookie crumbs from her fingers and onto her napkin. She stays for a few minutes more, asking some general questions about Micah's day care and our plans for Christmas break. I tell her about going to see Santa at the mall and going to the reading of *The Night Before Christmas* at the library. I tell her that Micah has asked for luna moths for his present, making her smile. I don't mention the trip we are going to make upstate in just a few days. The one that makes it hard to sleep at night. The one that has turned this whole family upside down. I walk Ms. Ballentine to the door, taking her headdress back before she pulls her coat back on.

"If you need anything, just call," she says, handing me her card. I fold my fingers around it and slide it into my back pocket. "Good luck," she says, smiling past me and toward the living room. I close the door behind her and close my eyes for a second. I know she means good luck with cleaning up the mess that has now taken over most of the front room, but I hope she means something bigger, because luck is something we've never had much of. I keep hoping as I follow the trail of crayons back into the living room that maybe our time has come for just a little bit of it. With just a little luck, maybe we can make it through.

CHAPTER EIGHTEEN

Shana

I ALWAYS FORGET how plain the hospital is, how ordinary.

You hear the words "mental institution" and you start thinking of some dark, gothic building with spires and gargoyles and stone walls. Kind of like the Bat Club, except not fake. But this place looks more like a retirement home, with one of those crappy wooden gazebos out front, and a lawn with brittle grass, and a fountain that never works, and lots of benches with buckets of sand sitting beside them, the sand sprouting cigarette butts like little gardens full of weeds. None of us has really talked on the way up, except Chloe showed Micah how to play car bingo, and she got mad at me for pointing out the water tower instead of letting him find it himself. The thing that really pissed me off is that the whole time Chloe's holding in her hand that same red piece of sea glass, rolling it in her fingers or hold-ing it in her cupped hands the way Catholic people hold their beads or crucifixes or whatever. And it's the same thing, really for her—a symbol of something she wants to believe in. But she's never seen. Everyone wants to see, right? Everyone wants proof, without thinking that maybe the proof will be for the thing you don't want to believe. The story of Mom that Chloe tells herself is no more true than the stories Mom used to tell us. And sea glass, when you think about it, is really just trash.

We pull into the parking lot and Dad says, "Well, here we are!" like we're stopping at Dairy Queen for ice cream. I think about making some big stand about staying in the car, but if Micah is going in, then I am, too. He leans up to look out the window, trying to figure out where we are—I know he can feel it, the way none of us can breathe, my heart slamming away inside my chest, Chloe's thumbs try-ing to wear away the sea glass.

Suddenly Chloe looks at me. "You didn't wear your bracelet," she says, the charms of her own bracelet clinking on her wrist.

I glance at her, then away. "No," I say, "I didn't."

"You should have."

Dad circles the parking lot again, around the plowed piles of dirty snow, looking for a spot. The radio advertises a carpet cleaning company, the singers sounding all too happy about the idea of spotless carpets.

"Yeah, you're right," I say. "We could add a new charm today. Like, a little patient strapped to a little gurney."

Her face darkens. "Shut up, Shana," she says, and it stings. I turned toward my own fogged-up window, my eyes burning.

"We don't say shut up," Micah says, but no one answers him.

We make our way through the automatic doors to where it's way too warm inside. It always is, but then you see the patients. All of them are wearing sweaters and shawls and knit hats, like old people. Except they're not. I mean, some are, but some are about as young as me and I bet most aren't even thirty yet. Everywhere it smells like some combination of cafeteria food and dirty people and too much baby powder. Dad goes over to the desk to sign us in and get our wristband IDs, and Chloe looks around at everything, and I can tell she is barely breathing. And neither am I. Micah doesn't have a clue, he just starts gathering up the little white stones in the base of the plastic plant, filling his pockets with them. At first it's kinda cute, but then I remember Virginia Woolf killed herself by filling her pockets with rocks and walking into the river, and so I make him dump them out. He cries for about two minutes, long enough for Chloe to say *nice job*, and then Dad walks over, all smiles, still holding the little teddy bear he brought along to give her, like she's some little kid in a cancer ward or something.

And he can't take it inside anyway, even I know that. There are all these rules, like you have to practically dress like a nun so that the freaks don't get all excited, and you have to go through a metal detector, and go directly to the visitation room—do not pass Go, do not collect two hundred dollars—and no food or drink or gum or anything, and don't have change jingling in your pocket or some patient will get upset because he wants it. I keep looking at the big steel doors, wondering how long it'll be before they call us back. Every so often there's some noise from back there, a shout, a cry. Chloe has to give up her bracelet and leave it behind the front desk. "Told you," I say to her.

I wander around the reception area while Chloe looks at some ladies magazine with Micah, pointing out pictures of food and kittens and toys. Down the hall toward the bathroom, I come across the one thing here that makes me happy—a poster. *My* poster, is how I think of it.

First off, this place has posters like most places have wallpaper, and they are all the bullshit "motivational" kind you see in school sometimes. But this one makes me laugh every time. There's this picture of an old red barn out in the middle of a hay field, with blue sky and clouds behind it, the barn leaning a little, the big doors open. Out to the side, in fancy script, it says, EVERY DAY, IN EVERY WAY, I'M GETTING BETTER AND BETTER. I saw it the first time we were here, when we were on the way down the hall to the visitation room, and it made me laugh out loud. I mean, what? Is the barn speaking? The barn is getting better and better? The best part, the whole time I was there, while Dad spoke in clichés and Mom spoke in nonsense, all I had to do was disappear inside myself, thinking about how that falling-down barn was getting better and better, instead of how my falling-down mother was not. I love that poster so much that I put my initials on it when no one was looking, and they're still there, in the corner, a little faded—S.L.B. Shana Lisa Beale. Shana Lisa, Shana Lisa . . . when I was little my dad used to sing it to me, from some old song about Mona Lisa, every night when I went to bed. . . .

"Shana Lisa, Shana Lisa, men have named you
You're so like the lady with the mystic smile"

Yeah, kind of a weird song for a little kid, and Dad couldn't carry a tune in a paper bag, but still some nights when I can't sleep I lie there and sing it to myself, just above a whisper, so I can barely hear it. I start to sing it now, under my breath, and then they call our names, ready to take us down to visitation.

Everything in the visitation room is bolted down. And I mean everything. The tables are bolted to the floor, and the chairs are bolted around the table, and the lamps are bolted to the end tables beside the couch, also bolted. The TV is bolted high on the wall, behind a Plexiglas screen so it can't get smashed, and the remote for the TV is bolted to the arm of the couch. Anything that can be broken or thrown doesn't exist in this room. There are no plants, no flowers, because patients will eat them. We sit around on the couches, waiting again, nervous with our hands, like we are on some collective first date or something. There is only one other patient with visitors right now (weekends are busiest), a young guy in a Patriots sweatshirt who sits staring at *The Price Is Right* on TV while his family—mom and dad, an aunt or two—ask him questions and then answer them when he doesn't. . . . *Much colder out, don't you think? . . . Yessir, it sure is colder.* He doesn't even move, just stares and stares at the game show. Maybe he is bolted down, too.

Then the doors next to the windows swing open, and a nurse steps through, and then Mom.

She smiles, right off, her eyes shiny and wet-looking, though I don't know if she's crying or just all drugged up and glassy. Dad stands up and hugs her and she smiles, patting his back, though she's just looking at the floor behind him. She's dressed weird, too, in a heavy sweater with a zipper and sneakers and jeans, stuff I have never seen before. She looks like she was dressed by someone else, in borrowed clothes. And the weirdest thing? All her long hair is pulled back behind this stupid-looking blue cap, the kind with mesh and a plastic adjuster, advertising Old Orchard Beach with a silhouette of a sunset in white. Right off Chloe starts crying and throws herself around Mom's waist with both arms, like she's the star of her own movie-of-the-week, and Mom pats her hair, pat pat pat, like a dog.

"My children," she says, her voice hoarse and croaky, but still her voice somehow, the same voice that used to ring through the house on Sunday mornings to call us to break-fast, and the same voice that used to tell us stories about the kings and queens under the sea, and the same voice that once told me how beautiful I was while we looked at me in the mirror. And for a moment I want to cry, too, except that whole bit is so whacked—*my children*, something she never in her life said, something else from a movie. Pretty much the whole thing feels like there's a script of it somewhere, and probably that's pretty much true. *Controlled environment*. That idea works great, except in the actual world.

"Shana," Dad says, "wouldn't you like to hug your mother?"

"Is that a rhetorical question?" I say to him, Mom smiling through the whole exchange. Dad and Chloe look at me like they want to kill me, and so I hug her the way you hug an aunt at a family reunion, and even the smell isn't her. She smells plastic. Then Micah hugs her. Just like that, he walks over and hugs her legs and then goes back to pushing at the lamp on the end table, baffled, I'm sure, that it won't budge. I mean, I don't get it. My fear, for all this time, has been that he is going to freak out and start screaming and screaming, the way he did that day, when I thought the screaming would never stop. And it didn't, except when his lungs emptied of air, and he was screaming with no noise. Now he's just sitting there, poking the bottom of his sneaker to make the red lights in the heel flash and blink.

"Well, so," Dad says, "how are you?" I can see him immediately regret the question. Chloe's beside me on the couch, and I can feel her stiffen up. Mom's nurse sits off to the side, pretending to read a magazine, pretending not to listen to us. She's wearing a Snoopy scrub top, which just depresses me. Everything around here has all this forced cheerfulness. Like if we wore Snoopy clothes at the mortuary on funeral days. At least our clothes admit that what goes on there is tragic, but not in this place.

"I started clozapine," she says, looking at our feet. "I think it's better." She looks up and smiles then, and for a second looks like herself, like any second she is going to take off the crappy clothes and have on her real clothes underneath, and laugh at how she fooled us all.

"Good, good," Dad says. His hands are shaking. He looks at us, his face drawn and desperate. "So," he says.

"I'm doing really well in school," Chloe says. "Almost all

A's last progress report." This is great, I think. The conversational equivalent of a letter to Grandma.

"Your nose," Mom says, looking right at me. At first I think she's talking about the fight, how bruised and swollen I was for days after, but that is long gone. I touch my nose, shaking my head, and touch the little amethyst stud there, the first step I took on my road to Gothdom.

"I pierced it," I tell her, then shrug. "No biggie."

She nods like she's already forgotten what we're talking about. "So, Micah—" she begins.

"You must watch a lot of game shows here," I say, just for some words to have, just to cut her off from talking to Micah. Chloe looks at me, and I shrug. Micah looks up from tying knots in his shoelaces and stares at her. He stares and stares while she thinks about the game show question, which, from the look on her face, is a complicated one. I watch him, and then it hits me—it's not that he's unafraid of her, he just doesn't know who she is. Somehow, mercifully, he doesn't remember. Mom tries hard to answer the game show question, or something, her face working through about fifty emotions. It's as if her face is trying to remember what it's supposed to look like.

"We're thinking you might like to come home sometime," Dad says. "A visit, to start."

"No way," I whisper. Chloe puts her hand on mine, then digs her nails into my skin, enough to hurt. I pull away from her, thinking about the time Mom told me that we all spend a half an hour as a single cell, and I wonder . . . if that's true, how does it come to this? So many people, hating themselves, hurting each other? Why does life complicate in the direction of what's bad?

"Can you stay?" Mom says to him.

"No, honey," he tells her. He rubs his mouth. "We have to leave here in an hour or so."

"But can you stay tonight?" she says. She puts her hand on his leg, and I notice her fingernails are all bitten down and dirty. They used to be longer, and the paint would collect under them, but they never looked dirty. She would hold them out and get me or Chloe to name the colors, like a box of crayons, except with more complicated names— viridian, Chinese white, cobalt, ochre.

"No, no," Dad says. "We can't, honey."

"Just some," Mom says, and she starts to breathe harder, like Micah does when he's about to cry. She pulls at the loose folds of her sweater. Behind us, I hear an audience clapping on TV. The nurse folds her magazine on her lap and watches us.

"You know," Chloe says, "Shana is going to be driving next year. I mean, look out, world." Dad makes himself laugh at this, and so do I.

Mom nods and smiles at me. "Look out, world," she says, and we all laugh again.

"Well," I say, and for the first time in over a year smile

back at her, "I will just try to drive when the world is doing something else." Micah sits beside me, busy pushing his socks down, then up, then down.

"Your nose," Mom says again, like she's forgotten already. She squints, trying to see it. "I don't think I like it."

Again I instinctively touch the little amethyst, and feel my face heating up. "It's just a thing I did," I tell her, and Dad nods, like I've said something profound.

"I don't like it," she says again, her voice flat. She leans way up in her seat to see it better, and when she does, I notice something I hadn't before—the Old Orchard Beach hat is one of those joke kind, covered across the bill with white splotches, made to look like birds have shit all over it. Suddenly I feel my heart slamming around inside me, and I want to stand up and run out of here. I mean, first they put her in this place, and then she has to live with all these freaks, and there is nothing but game shows on TV, and she has to wear clothes that look like they came out of the garbage, clothes other people were going to throw away anyway, and then as if all that weren't enough they put this goddam hat on her head. A shit hat, like my mother is some kind of a joke, like she's a house someone has egged.

"Mom," I say, "take that hat off."

She looks at me, her mouth working but with no sound.

"I mean it," I say. "Take that stupid hat off."

"Shana," Dad says, "it's no big deal if your mother doesn't like your pierced nose."

I shake my head. "No," I say, but it's too much to explain, and the sound inside my ears is like water rushing down a drain and I can feel myself sweating under my coat and all I want is out of there. "Take it *off*," I say, and reach to grab it, miss.

"Shana," Chloe says. "Leave her alone."

I know they are all waiting for her to freak out, and the nurse says something about how our time is almost up, but Mom just looks at me, really looks at me, like she sees me, like some door inside her has blown open for a half a minute, and then she calmly, quietly, reaches up and takes off her hat.

And when she does, all her blond hair spills out from under and behind it, sliding in thick curtains around her shoulders, and Micah looks up, and he starts screaming, the sound just pouring out of him like his lungs are tearing in two, and the nurse jumps up, telling us we will have to leave now, and Chloe is on her knees in front of the couch saying *Micah, Micah, Micah*, over and over again, holding him, and Dad just sits there stunned, trying to speak. Mom looks at Micah for a few moments, just stares at him, and then she is out of her seat, running toward the steel doors, doubled over, her shins banging into the furniture, and then the nurse is up and after her, grabbing her from behind, telling us to go now, and I don't know what to do, what to look at, and so I look at nothing and everything all at once, at Micah rocking in Chloe's arms, at my hands curled like dead things in my lap, at Dad with the color drained from his face, at the other family turning back to their game show, at Chloe looking at me over Micah's shoulder like she wishes I were dead, at all the bolts holding everything down, and at Mom's hat, sitting on the floor under her chair, that joke of a hat, all covered in shit. The steel doors close, and like that, Mom is gone again.

CHAPTER NINETEEN

Chloe

"YOU JUST COULDN'T stand it, could you?" I had managed to keep my mouth shut the whole way home—six and a half minutes to find a bathroom for Micah and help him get a drink at the water fountain and get into the car. Another three to make it out of the parking lot. Fifty-eight minutes until we made it onto Exchange Street. Seven more before we made it into our apartment and all headed off in different directions. Dad to the roof. Micah into the kitchen. Shana to her bedroom. That's where I find her—headphones jammed in her ears, the scratchy whispering of music floating out of her earbuds, like someone arguing, low and fast and hard. Shana looks over at me slowly then just shakes her head and closes her eyes again. I pick up the closest thing I can find, her blue glass piggy bank—a twin to the amber one in my room—and hold it high over my head. I look back over at her again, but she still has her eyes closed. "Shana." I say it loud, nearly yelling. She still won't open her eyes.

It's funny when you decide to do something that you know is wrong, that you know might hurt someone or something. It's as if all this heat gets built up inside of you and the noise in your head gets louder and louder and the pressure behind your eyes gets so intense that you know if you don't do the thing, if you back down, you might just die or go crazy. And it's in that last moment before you either do it or not that you can see the place deep inside yourself. The pure you that no one and nothing can touch, that even you don't know about. It's the you that you were born with. The you that didn't get messed up when no one came to your fifth birthday party and didn't get muddied when you overheard your best friend tell everyone on the bus that your mom was crazy. It's the you that stays you while all the other stuff just gets folded around it, hiding it and pressing in on it until no one can even see you at all. It's at that moment that you get to see what you really are and what you can be and what you can't be. I feel my fingers pressing into the glass of the piggybank. I can close my eyes and see it shattering into a million pieces all over the floor. I can hear the initial crash and then the softer tinkling as each piece finds its own resting place. I can feel the tendons in my hand start to let go, start to pull my fingers back one at a time. Then Shana opens her eyes.

+ + +

Chloe

The painting should have warned us. The one of Shana was done all in golds and oranges, her eyes nearly as intense on the canvas as in real life. Mine was all blues and greens and purples, my hair twisting around me like seaweed. It was Micah's, the unfinished one, that was wrong. It was his that should have shaken us awake. It was his that told us how bad it was. From the start, it seemed off, the colors all wrong. The face only a smudge at first that only got worse the longer she worked on it. Where his skin should have been clear and soft, it was broken and scarred. Where his hands should have been curved and small, they were huge and sharp and dangerous. But even all of that might have been okay. Might have been explained away. It was the eyes that couldn't be ignored. Where Micah's eyes are deep and blue and clear, the eyes in the painting, Micah's eyes, were just holes. Black and bottomless and empty.

"Don't," Shana says, pulling the headphones from her ears. "Please." I lower the piggy bank to my chest, cradling it in my arms. Shana sits up and scoots back, leaning her back against the headboard. "Just say it," she says so softly I can barely hear her.

"Say what?" I ask, thinking a million things I'd like to say. Like she just ruined our chance for a normal Christmas. Say she wrecked the first visit I've had with Mom in over a year. Tell her that Micah is now about seven handfuls into a box of Lucky Charms, trying to find happiness in a rainbow of colored marshmallows. Ask her what the hell she was thinking when she scared Mom and freaked out Micah and made Dad cry and made me feel like slapping her. "What do you want me to say?" I ask, my voice shaking. "You want me to tell you that you ruined everything? That you and your anger and your hostility are breaking this family apart?" I am practically shouting now, and I can hear the coins rattle slightly inside the piggy bank that I am still clutching. "What am I supposed to say, Shana?"

"I don't know," she whispers. She swipes at her hair that has fallen across her cheek. I can see the blond roots starting to grow in along her part, nearly an inch-wide stripe of yellow in the midst of the black. She tucks her hair behind her ear and swipes at her cheek again, this time at the tears that have started winding their way down to her chin.

"Don't you dare," I say. She looks up at me, her eyes wet and red. "You-are-not-allowed-to-cry-about-this." I say each word separately, making space in between them for my anger to push through.

"And why is that, Chloe?" she asks. She isn't whispering anymore. "Do you have some sort of monopoly on feeling sad in this family?" She swipes at her eyes again and sits forward. "Do you think you're the only one who misses Mom? Who misses having anything resembling a normal life?" I shake my head and watch as she pushes herself off the bed. "As far as I know there are three children in this family. Not one." She steps toward me, stopping just out of reach. "You aren't the only one who's hurting."

"I never thought—"

"No, that's right. You didn't think. You didn't think about how any of this works."

"If that's right, Shana, then tell me. Share with me how all of this works. Tell me why you keep acting like Mom doesn't exist. Tell me why you don't want her coming here."

"No," Shana says much more softly. "You tell me why."

"How the hell should I know? All I know is that every time Mom comes up you start acting all squirrelly and you walk around tearing up stockings and slicing up paintings. . . ." Shana looks up at me. I nod and watch as she bites at the corner of her lip. "All I know is you ripped Mom's hat off and you made Micah cry."

"I didn't make Micah cry," Shana says, looking up at me. "Mom did."

"How did she—" I keep looking at Shana and I can feel the floor tilt under me. I put my hand out to grab at the dresser, forgetting that I am holding the piggy bank. I watch as it slips forward, tipping toward the floor. It balances for a moment on the ends of my fingers, an impossible display of grace, before tipping farther. Tipping too far. Floating away from my hand into thin air, turning slowly twice as it falls.

+ + +

JARS *of* GLASS

The rolling lights of the ambulance danced across the chipped marble columns. I could hear loud voices upstairs. First Dad's, then Mom's, then Shana's. Beneath all of that was a softer noise, one I couldn't place until I was nearly right on top of them. Micah. He was so still, lying on the stretcher. One arm tucked in against his side, the other folded across his stomach, a mass of white bandages twisted around it. The noise was only slightly louder when I was right next to him. A soft whimper, quiet and gentle. He turned to look at me, his blue eyes so bright in the afternoon sunlight. "*Chlo-ee*," he whispered. They rolled him past me and toward the service elevator. I could hear Shana and Dad talking fast and hard. Words like "burned" and "accident" and "stove." A fireman stood in front of them, his suspenders hanging down his back like broken wings. He kept patting my mother on the shoulder, telling her that Micah would be fine. I could only see her from the side, her long gold hair falling across her face.

"Ellie," my father said, pulling her toward him. "It's okay. It was an accident." She let herself be pulled forward, almost losing her balance as she fell into him. He reached over to pull Shana in, too, lifting his other hand toward her. She stepped back, her arms folded, her face hard. She looked past my father toward where I was standing in the doorway. She held my gaze for a moment before walking past our parents, past the fireman, and toward me. She stopped for a moment, watching my face, searching for something, then she walked past. Barely brushing against me with her shoulder and then gone.

We stand in the midst of the broken piggy bank, listening as the last of the tiny pieces of blue slowly spin away from us, finding their rest in the shadows under the bed, in the cracks between the floorboards, in the hidden places in the dark. Shana steps toward me and I hear the crunch of glass under her boot.

"I just thought it was an accident," I say, but I can feel the truth pushing at me. "His hand," I say, letting Shana put her arms around me. "His tiny hand." I lean my face into her shoulder, feeling the softness of her hair against my cheek. She presses her hands against my back, pulling me into her, letting me sink against her. We stand like that for what feels like forever, leaning against each other, feeling the warmth of each of our bodies push into the other. We lean against each other, finding a quiet warm place in the midst of a cold sea of broken glass.

CHAPTER TWENTY

Shana

VERNON SAYS WE are in the right business, he and I, because death is more popular than ever before.

It's about all I could think about at Christmas, and who could blame me? I mean, Christmas Day we had two people come in downstairs—the first a ninety-year-old guy who died of lung cancer even though he never smoked, and the second a fifteen-year-old girl who died of a defective heart during basketball practice and made the evening news. I mean, that's the whole story of Christmas, isn't it? A birth that implies a death? Then again, every birth implies a death, pretty much. Santa Claus and the mall are just ways of distracting ourselves from that. I guess that's our story, too, a family that was born out of two people loving each other, then one of the people died, at least her mind did, and motherhood died in the time it took for a little boy's hand to be pushed against a stove, and then marriage died, and so the family died.

After our visit, we didn't even try for a Christmas, and I honestly think Dad forgot what day it was anyway. He spent the day on the roof, bundled up in a down parka, smoking. Since that day, things have been weird with Chloe, like she was mad at me for the truth of everything, or maybe we were like my piggy bank—good luck gluing it back together. You've got maybe a million pieces, and some of those disappeared down the heating vents. Gone. Pieces of us are gone, too. She tried, Chloe did. I mean, Christmas afternoon she gave me a wrapped present that turned out to be a pair of wool socks. I told her it was the kind of present an orphan would get, and she just shook her head and took them back. We gave Micah a box of Lucky Charms and let him spend the day watching a SpongeBob DVD. Chloe gave her jars of sea glass to Raven, mostly because she just didn't want them anymore. Dad gave Vernon the entire business, without even knowing it. I gave Jason a long kiss when we took a walk around the docks on Christmas afternoon, the only things open a Chinese restaurant and the pool hall, which never closes. I gave Chloe distance. I wanted to give Dad a carton of Marlboros, but even I am not enough of a smart-ass to do that. I gave Mom a silent promise that she would never come home, not as long as we lived here, and I know Chloe made the same vow after that day she smashed my piggy bank. So we agreed on something, at least.

I didn't know what to think about us.

So, what happened? Well, Raven gets word that our Christmas Day was like something Charles Dickens might have invented when he was having a really bad day, and she said, according to Chloe, "That just won't do."

"What does that mean?" I asked her.

Chloe just shrugged. "I don't know," she said. "She said it wouldn't do, then she thanked me for the sea glass, then Sean said, no, that wouldn't do at all."

More and more Chloe was over there with them, moving away from here. First Mom; then Dad; now Chloe and Micah hanging out with Raven and Izzy and Sean, all moving away from me. I'm left with the Vernon Show, but Vernon is actually seventy-five years old, I found out when we were doing payroll, and so when he goes, then what? Jason, right, because everyone knows that high school romances last forever. Cheerleaders think that. I know better. Nothing lasts forever—add that to the collection of Clichés That Turn Out to Be True.

It's like a home invasion, with snack mix.

Six o'clock on New Year's Eve, and we've just finished eating hot dogs and waffle fries, and Jason is washing dishes after I scrape them, and I am half wondering if everyone will be down at the Bat Club tonight, hanging out and partying, but realizing, too, that I can't do it anymore. The black-and-white—somehow, I just don't want to disappear anymore, because I think the next time I do I won't make it back, I'll just cease to exist. That, and I don't want to stand around with all my angst and sorrow, posing with it like it's a bendable action figure. Pull the string, hear a litany of boredom. Real sorrow, I've found out, doesn't need any costumes. I guess Jason doesn't either, or maybe he just doesn't want it because I don't, and if so, that makes me like him even more. Anyway, I am thinking about that while I swipe the counters with a sponge, while Chloe ties up the garbage and talks to Vernon, who more and more often comes by for dinner. Only tonight he came by to offer her a job, afternoons, dusting the pews, watering the plants, all the stuff I was doing just a few months before.

She shrugs. "Sure," she says. "What do I have to do?" And right then there is a loud knock at the door, and without missing a beat Vernon says, "Let's see how your door-opening skills hold up," and then, there they are, all of them—Raven and Izzy and Sean and some guy named Todd I have never met before, and they are carrying bags of stuff, food and noisemakers and soda and a big cake with a frosting clock on it, the hands set at midnight. They all shout *Happy New Year!* as loud as they can, and I swear it seems like fourteen people coming through the door instead of just four, and right away Micah is after the cake and so is Izzy, and it's like, what the hell, give it to them, give them all the cake they want, and the boys, all shy, are shaking hands with Vernon like he's our dad or something, and right off Vernon tells them he's been wondering some-thing . . . if a deaf kid swears, does his mother wash his hands with soap? Sean and Todd cut their eyes at me, and I tell them if they want to hang around here, they'd better get used to it.

By sometime after eleven o'clock Micah and Izzy are asleep on the couch under his Spider-Man blanket, his hand with the scar curled up under his chin, Izzy's curls spilling over his shoulder and into the plate of fudge still perched on his lap. For half an hour the two of them ran around in circles shouting "Happy New Year!" over and over, throwing whatever they could find into the air. I know that as young as he is, Micah likely won't remem-ber much of this past year, won't remember what happened. But someday, he will be thinking about that scar on his hand, and he'll ask me, ask Chloe. And right this second, I know one thing—we're going to lie to him, give him a perfect, beautiful lie he can hang on to as tightly as he is hanging on to that blanket, and never have to know what happened. Some things have their own right and wrong, already built in.

Jason wraps his arms around me from behind and whispers *Happy New Year* against my ear, kisses the side of my neck. I lean back against him, then turn my head to kiss him.

"You're a little early," I tell him.

I feel him smile. "I wanted to be first. Besides, I never

told you that before, so I owe you about fourteen of them, one for every year we missed."

I smile, too. "Maybe we shouldn't count prelanguage infancy . . . you couldn't have said it then anyway."

"'Prelanguage infancy.' Man, you are such a romantic."

I smile again, just looking around me. Sean has his guitar out and is singing weepy, heartfelt versions of every TV commercial jingle that comes on, making everyone laugh. Right now he is closing his eyes, as if in anguish, his voice straining in a hoarse whisper about some kind of aluminum foil that makes life better. Todd is arguing that the Vulcan salute is actually based on a sign of blessing given by Jewish priests, though no one but Vernon is really listening to him. Chloe and Raven are stringing lights, Christmas lights, through the whole place, the big, fat colored bulbs, not the weenie little white ones, and Chloe is laughing so much that it makes me feel like I am watching old videos—I can't remember the last time she laughed like that. She is also starting to paint again, though I'm not supposed to know it. Jason squeezes my waist once more and whispers that he'll be right back, he is going for more ginger ale, and I just stand still, watching, thinking how it must look from the outside, how strange, the top of the mortuary spilling out all this light and warmth and laughter and noise. It almost makes me wish I were just passing by on the sidewalk, just looking up and smiling, but when I think about outside, suddenly I remember Dad, out there on the rooftop.

I open the window, and at first I can't really make him out. It's snowing now, the big, fat flakes that fall slowly and seem to drop silence down on the whole world. Then I see the movement of his arm, lifting a bottle to his mouth as he leans back in a lawn chair, bundled up in his parka, his feet propped up on the air-conditioning vents.

"Dad?" I call as loud as I can. The rooftop is glossy black, frozen. "Dad?" I say again, and I think I see him wave toward me, but I can't really tell. I take one step out on the roof, but it's too slippery, and more than that, he doesn't want me out there. He wants to be left alone.

"Hey, they're going to drop the ball," I shout. "Come on in."

He waves again, or at least his silhouette does, and I step back in the window and just watch him for a minute, his black silhouette, the white snow falling all around him, smoke from his cigarette rising in clouds around him, and I realize—he is like I was for so long, disappearing into the black and white. If he would just turn his head, he could see a world of color, all of us in here, waiting for him to come back, but he has to do that, we can't do it for him. I know that better than anyone. I call to him once more, watching him lift his hand in a slow wave, then close the window on all that cold and dark.

"Hurry *up*," Chloe says to me, grabbing my hand from out of nowhere. She drags me into the living room, where they have started the countdown on TV, the ball making its slow way down the pole while people cheer and blow air horns and the corner of the screen counts down the seconds in big yellow numbers. We all stand around it, counting with the TV, making our voices louder and louder, those big, fat bulbs spilling color and light over all of us. For a second my mind moves across all of us, Mom and Dad and Micah and Chloe and everything that has happened to us, all the ways we have broken, but then the idea comes to me that maybe the reverse is true, too, maybe every death implies a birth. Something new, and full of promise. We all wrap our arms around each other like some goofy chorus line as the last seconds tick down, even Vernon, smiling and counting for all he is worth, and Chloe's hand finds mine, our fingers interlacing as the time runs out, the ball ends its drop, everything blazes into light and noise, and in the space of a second, the time it takes Chloe to squeeze my hand, something old becomes something new.